Saving
DEE

L.H. WILLIAMS

About The Author

L. H. Williams is a pseudonym for Louise and Heyward Williams, a young-at-heart married couple who found each other again after many years apart. They discovered they shared a love of writing that had begun decades ago in junior high school, where they both studied under the watchful eye of BCHS's much-loved English teacher, Doris Pock. They found that writing was the perfect hobby for them, since it gave them an outlet for their vivid imaginations. Louise was the lover of romantic fiction and Heyward liked to immerse himself in adventure novels.

Thus began a partnership of long talks and a can-do attitude that resulted in the manuscript of *Saving Dee*. Never having written a novel before, they decided they needed a professional editor to give their story some polish. Happily they found Nikki Busch, a talented editor of award-winning fiction, who was willing to take on the task of working with two unknowns on their first literary work. Not only did she edit, she also taught them how to hone their craft and develop their technical skills. In the process they became friends, and most recently she finished editing their second novel, which will be published shortly.

Meanwhile, the pair is hard at work on their third novel.

Dear Reader,

We have enjoyed writing this light-hearted romance and adventure story and hope you enjoy reading it. After the Epilogue you will find an introduction to our second novel, **The Penny Scam**, which continues the escapades of our fun-loving and totally fictional cast of characters.

~ Louise and Heyward

Prologue

JARED SMILED AND MOVED A pawn forward to threaten Stanley's bishop. Stanley looked at it for a minute and then gently tipped his king over. "Damn!" he said.

They were in Stanley's Georgetown lodgings, having a postprandial Armagnac and playing chess after a delightful dinner. Stanley leaned back and said, "When am I going to stop underestimating you? You come up with the most unexpected moves. I had you three moves back and I still lost."

"I had you five moves back. It was just a matter of time."

Stanley had a top government job defining and enforcing the International Trade in Arms Regulations, otherwise known as ITAR. Jared had met him while working to comply with these regulations on behalf of some foreign clients. They'd bonded over a common dissatisfaction with the way national security interests were handled and over the years they had formed a solid friendship. They trusted each other implicitly.

Stanley leaned back in his chair, sipped his Maison Gelas '45, and regarded Jared.

"Jared, my friend, you might be just the person to help me in a somewhat contiguous but unrelated problem. My wife has a friend whose sister is married to a 'person of interest.' The request came back up the food chain, and I, unfortunately, happened to be the chef du jour. Now I am supposed to find the truth, exculpate the husband or extricate the sister, all without disturbing the status quo and without anyone knowing that I am involved. That is, without any official intercession. Can you help?"

1

Jared gave him a long, thoughtful look and then a twinkle of amusement settled in his eyes. "Tell me about the sister."

"Her name is Dee."

Chapter 1

Dee

DOROTHY BARBARA WHEATON, OTHERWISE KNOWN as Dee, was smart, and she hid it well, most likely a carryover from her high school days when girls were either smart or popular. Even now, in her thirties, Dee continued with the charade. She'd finished high school near the top of her class, and in college she'd earned her fine arts degree with little effort. She excelled at the courses that required endless hours of reading followed by writing papers filled with critical analyses of some obscure point. She'd done the required reading with her feet up in a remote corner of a quiet student lounge, and the papers were efficiently written and typed while she worked at an endless parade of part-time jobs. Now, four years into her second marriage, Dee acknowledged that she was still playing dumb, and it irritated her.

In fact, she noted that the dumbing down was now complete, if you considered how she had molded herself to please her husband, Steve. "What a jerk he is," she mused. "I thought he was a successful businessman and that we'd find things in common, but it's nothing like that." So, she found herself dressing like a hussy, a far cry from the sophisticated look she'd worn with such pride. Steve liked her to look flashy, so she was his makeover from head to toe, from her platinum hair to her bejeweled, strappy gold sandals. And the fact that she'd once managed a successful midtown art gallery was lost amid a round of dinners with Steve and his clients: dinners at which she was expected to keep her mouth shut and act impressed with her husband's business acumen. She wondered idly how she'd fallen so low.

She reminded herself that it was just over a decade since she'd graduated college, her head so full of ideas for conquering the New York City art world that she was sure she'd be an instant success. Instead she'd found a low-paying job with a tyrant of a boss, and in the same year she married the boy she'd dated in college. They never had an engagement. He simply showed up one weekend saying he missed her and asked if she would marry him. Living the lonely life of an underpaid New York gofer, Dee accepted, and Andy moved into her two-room walkup. It never worked from the beginning, but Dee was too stubborn to admit it for the first two years. She decorated the ugly apartment with art prints on the walls and colorful pottery on the tables, but she couldn't do anything about her husband. He had never grown up, so the sex was pity sex and the conversations were all about motivating Andy to do something with his life. Before she knew it, Dee was divorced and living alone again.

But this time it was different. After two years of what felt like pushing around a large inanimate object, she felt a surge of inner energy and drive and focused on her career with the same energy that had gotten her through high school and college. With perfect timing, the gallery's owner fired the tyrant and made her the new manager. Then he left for Europe to find new artists, leaving her in charge. Anticipating the extra money in her paycheck, Dee purchased an elegant business suit and a gorgeous pair of stilettos. On the first Monday morning in her new role, she was poised and confident, and it showed. She already knew her art, so it was simply a matter of taking good care of her customers, and she knew how to do that, too.

There was a rhythm to the art scene in New York City. During the day it was the usual tourist trade, the art world's equivalent of tire kickers. They were looking for a piece to hang over the couch in their Iowa home, and Dee would sell them a painting of the perfect size and color and have it shipped to them. Lunch hours and after work were devoted to the up-and-comers, the yuppies furnishing their flats with works by artists they hoped would someday be famous. But at night out came the wealthy art lovers, those patrons of the arts who knew instinctively what was worthy of collecting, even if the artist was still an unknown. They strolled in, the hetero and the gay couples, the elderly and the young. Dee recognized them by the serious nature of their conversations, the way they walked from room to room, from painting to painting, whispering with their heads bent toward to each other. Only then, after much discussion, would they approach her to talk about an acquisition.

She endured the day's customers; she treasured the nights at the gallery. She loved the way these special clients revered art and knew what they loved. There was a sense of awe in the way they approached their searches, and the way they demonstrated a quiet appreciation of the works pleased her soul. It did not take long before Dee had quite a following among the city's art lovers. They appreciated her genteel approach to dealing with her customers, noted how she remembered their special likes and dislikes, and loved the way she brought in special pieces for them to view. Business was booming, and it was all because of Dee. In the space of two years she'd gone from gofer to successful art gallery manager.

It was at home that she felt the loneliness. Night after night, curled up on the bed with only a book for company, she began to feel the walls closing in. Going out with friends was expensive, so after she repeatedly turned down their invites, they stopped asking her to join them. And without this entry into the social whirl of the city, Dee had no way to meet the very gentlemen who might enjoy her company. It was a catch-22. Her income was enough to keep the roof over her head but not enough for her to enjoy the best that New York City had to offer—its amazing nightlife. Besides, by the time she got home, she was too tired to do much. At times, she thought of returning to upstate New York and looking for a job there. But she wasn't quite willing to let go of her dream. *No,* she thought, *not quite yet.*

Then one night Steve strolled in, all swagger and attitude. Dee knew in an instant he was not part of the usual night scene. She was not sure what he was, exactly, but her mind went to "nouveau riche." Steve immediately picked out two items in the gallery—a large abstract painting to hang over the couch in his newly acquired industrial loft—and Dee. He invited her to join him the next night for dinner and drinks after work, and from then on proceeded to woo her with all his considerable worth.

Chapter 2

Steve

STEVE MILANESSI WAS BORN IN Boston's north end to second-generation immigrants who owned a grocery supply business. He was the second of two sons and had three younger sisters who married early and produced a horde of grandchildren, which greatly pleased his parents. His older brother went to work in the distribution end of the business, but Steve wasn't interested in trucking food all over New England. He wanted to make money. Lots of money. He had noticed early on that his father regularly gave one of his friends a thick envelope of cash. "That's just insurance," his father told him. Steve was not stupid and it didn't take him long to figure out what that meant.

His good looks and his rebellious nature attracted the young ladies in his neighborhood. He made his first conquest at age fifteen with the daughter of one of his father's friends; unfortunately, she became pregnant. His father was furious and threatened to beat him to death, but by then he knew that Steve wouldn't stand for it. Money changed hands and the problem was resolved. Then Steve did it again and more money changed hands. The girl was forced to seduce a somewhat dim-witted boy who was told he was the father and had to marry her. Once again, Steve was off the hook. By now he was too grown up—and too strong—to let his father beat him. But, when one of his father's insurance friends took Steve aside, tied him up, and left him out in the snow overnight, Steve got the message.

7

By the time he was nineteen, he had established himself as the accountant of the business; he was doing the buying and selling, and he expanded it by importing goods from abroad. With the help of his "insurance agents" he eliminated some of his competitors. The agents reported back that they thought he was ready. So he was set up.

It started when his brother had to make a delivery to Roxbury because his driver mysteriously didn't show up. He was badly beaten and the goods were stolen by a group of locals. Steve was incensed and went to his agents for assistance. They assured him they would find out who did it, although they already knew— they'd set the locals up as well, because they'd been a pain in the ass for too long. The agents figured they could kill two birds with one stone.

Steve was given a crowbar and accompanied by three large gentlemen to a bar, which immediately cleared out except for the small group of locals in the back. When they noticed Steve, one of them said, "Want some of what your bro got?" Steve went after him like a shot and broke his right knee with his first swing. His companions were up and swearing, when they noticed the three large gentlemen—and their guns—and their expressionless faces. Steve broke the other knee and the left elbow, which was unfortunate because up to that time the man had been left-handed. One of the gentlemen finally hauled Steve off and they left.

They took him to an expensive apartment he'd never seen before and explained to him that he'd passed a very important test. He was now "in," and "out" was not an option.

Steve agreed. "What do you want me to do?"

"Expand your import-export business," came the response from Steve's newly acquired benefactor.

So he did. He had already been importing (smuggling) Iranian caviar along with some other very expensive delicacies. He had judiciously been giving his benefactor a percentage of the profits rather than a fixed premium, only reporting what he claimed he earned to his father, while keeping the rest for himself. But now he told his benefactor that he had to legitimize the business to keep his father clean, and he wanted to move to New York City to be "where the action is."

"Very commendable about your father; a son should show respect. And I don't mind if you leave Boston. I can still watch over you if you're in New York. But what about the caviar? I've acquired a taste for it!"

Steve replied in Arabic that it would still be coming in but from a different route.

"What did you say?"

Steve translated—and the fact that he'd learned another language to facilitate his business was not lost on the benefactor.

"There are other things that can be exported."

"I've already got three shadow corporations set up and importing. They can export as well."

"Three? I only know about one!"

"Good. If you couldn't find the other two, then neither will the government."

Over the next decade Steve became wealthy. His benefactor was pleased, because his cash reserves grew in equal measure to Steve's. Sometimes he wondered whether he deserved an even larger share, but then he thought about the good life he was leading and how it would be a shame to spoil the sweetness of it all. He mused about the parody of killing the goose that laid the golden egg and enjoyed his caviar, along with a luxurious lifestyle.

In the meantime, Steve's wealth accumulated at such a rapid pace he could hardly spend it fast enough. Not one to waste much time thinking about these things, Steve began a round of acquisitions. He sold his first apartment, and with the help of a sexy real-estate agent in New York, he bought, renovated, and decorated a large penthouse loft. He'd walked through it three times: the day he screwed his agent on the hardwood floor, the day he plunked down the cash to buy it, and the day he moved in five months later.

He then turned his attention to relaxation, something he rarely enjoyed, and decided he needed a yacht. He used the same MO he'd used to purchase the apartment—wads of cash and a sexy broker. He was more interested in bedding the ladies than he was in selecting the merchandise. If he had to expend his energy on something other than his business dealings, it might as well be in sexual pleasures. His appetites were legendary in the parts of the city where he operated and the chosen ladies were always flattered by his attention, fleeting as it was. There were no illusions among them; they knew Steve and his prowess and took him at face value.

One night, coming home from a business meeting in Manhattan, Steve's limo was stopped in traffic across from a well-lit art gallery. One look at the leggy lady in the window and he told the driver to wait for him. He sauntered in, all swagger and attitude and told the blonde he needed a really large work of art for his new loft. He left with two things: an expensive canvas and the promise of a date with Dee.

He decided that Dee was "class" and that he needed to clean up his act if he wanted to get anywhere with her. So he went back to the one place he knew where he might get a "quick and dirty" education: his old neighborhood and the hooker who dated rich guys. He was a quick study. In two evenings, which were only partly classes in manners, Steve refreshed himself on the "dos and dont's" of taking a classy lady out to dinner.

His first date with Dee was only a partial success, but Steve wasn't one to overanalyze these things. He knew he'd talked too much, but he did need to let her know how successful he was. After all, if he didn't tell her, who would? The view from the rooftop restaurant was gorgeous, and so was Dee. He could tell she'd dressed her best, and she seemed impressed. Steve asked her out again, and she accepted, but she pulled away when he brought her back to her building; he was left kissing the air as she darted inside.

What Steve saw over the next few weeks was a woman who fit beautifully into the world he was introducing her to. She appeared to be at ease in the most expensive places, and her face glowed in the lights of fancy restaurants and nightspots. She carried herself with grace and never let on that all of this was new to her. But what Steve couldn't know was that Dee was rapidly being seduced by the lifestyle; he thought she was crazy about him.

Alone in her apartment at night, Dee took off the fancy clothes and prepared for the next day's work at the gallery. She was tired from the late nights and knew that the double life she was leading could not go on forever. She looked around at her flat and thought how easy it would be to walk away from it all. After seven years in this rent-controlled, third-floor walkup, all that was worth taking from this life fit into two suitcases. She prepared herself mentally for the good things in her future, but she also understood the price she would have to pay for it.

It took Steve three months to convince her to marry him. On the night she accepted his engagement ring, he took her down to Atlantic City in the limo. She'd packed a small overnight bag and knew she couldn't stall the inevitable any longer. He was becoming harder to put off, and she was running out of excuses. She was not physically attracted to him, but she had to admit he was a powerful man, and powerful men did have their own attraction, didn't they?

He had ordered dinner sent to the suite, and when the waiter removed the silver covers, she saw her favorites were on the menu. After several succulent courses and three glasses of champagne, she finally slid reluctantly into bed with the greedy and over-ready Steve, who wasted no time in bedding his fiancée.

Through her champagne haze Dee found herself responding to his ministrations. What Steve lacked in sexual subtlety, he made up with vigor and enthusiasm. He used all of his legendary prowess on her, and her body began to respond in spite of herself.

"My beauty, my beauty," Steve said as he lowered himself onto her, ignoring the faint look of apprehension in her eyes. But he had taken his time with her, making sure she was ready for him. He knew he could carry on all night and wondered idly how long his intended would be able to match his stride. He was still eager for more when she begged him to let her sleep.

He quickly dressed once she'd fallen asleep and went in search of a hooker. He was back in the room beside Dee when she stirred and asked what time breakfast would be served.

It took Dee less than six months of marriage to realize her mistake, but by then it was too late.

Steve was, in short, a piece of work. His smooth surface covered a multitude of sins, including a bad temper and an unbending, unrelenting arrogance. Combined with his basic ignorance of human behavior, it was the perfect storm for bad dealings with his customers and for ugly scenes with Dee. He never backed down, never admitted he was wrong, never apologized, and never, ever, gave anyone the benefit of the doubt. Early on he made her quit her job at the gallery to devote herself entirely to his needs. But his needs went way beyond the confines of marriage, and she never forgave him for that.

Worse, she blamed herself for her own short-sighted decision to marry. On bad days she was depressed; on good days she used her wealth to give herself some short-term pleasure. At least, she thought, she was impeccably groomed and expensively dressed.

Not a bad life for a prisoner with an enormous loft in Soho and a fifty-four-foot yacht in Miami.

Jared sat at the bar in an exclusive restaurant high above New York City, surreptitiously watching Steve and his friends… and Dee. He had read the dossiers Stanley provided, but this was the first time he'd seen them all in person. Steve was what he'd expected: loud, brash, flaunting his wealth and success; his friends were the same. Jared noticed one of them sneaking puzzled glances at him. He remembered having saved the owner of a great little tech company from that very same shark and wondered if he'd been recognized. Jared slowly turned around, and for the remainder of the evening he observed the group by watching them in the mirror behind the bar.

Dee was another story entirely. He knew about her childhood, her first unsuccessful marriage, her job at the art gallery and her marriage to Steve. Now he watched her and used his experience in judging people to understand her. She appeared polite; she laughed at Steve's jokes at the right time and smiled at his business associates when appropriate. He also heard Steve brag that "me and Dee" were going on a vacation on their yacht in Miami. Jared made a mental note of this, knowing that his own yacht was in Fort Lauderdale. He watched as one of the associates, who seemed slightly intoxicated, put his hand on Dee's knee, and a large gentleman quickly put a stop to that.

"Okay," said Jared, "That man's security, and Steve must have reason for it."

As he studied Dee he sensed the unhappiness behind her smile. Watching until they left, he quickly punched the speed dial for Stanley on his cell phone.

"I'm in," was all he said.

Chapter 3

Labor Day Weekend – September 2008

DEE PICKED HER WAY DOWN the long wooden dock, her eyes squinting against the sun, her heels clicking rhythmically on the wood. She was aware that men working on their boats would stop what they were doing to look at her long, shapely legs. She worked her way around the coiled ropes, tackle boxes and coolers being unloaded from the yachts.

As she walked back from the marina shops, she thought for the tenth time that day that Steve was not an easy man to live with. Sure, he handed her cash and told her to get her hair done and buy herself something nice, but he didn't talk to her. The topic of business was off-limits and his past was a closed book. *That doesn't leave much, does it?* She sighed. It was a business deal, not a marriage.

Three days ago they had flown first class from New York to Miami with the idea of taking the entire week of Labor Day as a long-overdue vacation, but ever since their arrival in the Miami Marina Steve had been on the phone. The boat she was headed to was a fifty-four-foot yacht named the *Esmeralda* that Steve had purchased not long before he met Dee.

The cruiser swayed in the wake of a passing boat as Dee returned. She dumped her packages, kicked off her sandals, and went below to find Steve.

"Where have you been?" he asked tersely. "I need to get some dinner."

She felt as though he'd hit her, so negative was his presence.

14

"Sure, honey, that's a great idea," she answered brightly. "Maybe you'd like a lobster or a seafood salad?"

He started to answer her when his cell phone rang again. She reached for the open wine bottle, poured herself a glass, and added a little to Steve's in response to his impatient gesture.

"No, that's not what I said to do at all." His voice was more like a growl as he spoke. "You dummy, I told you: it's a wording trick on the bill of sale and the other papers. It's just electronics, you know—not rocket science! Change some of the wording to make it look like the stuff's different; you know, approved stuff, legal stuff. Oh, you know what I mean. Do I have to spell it out for you?"

He looked around, as though to see if Dee was listening. When she hid herself from view, she heard him say gruffly, "Yes, we need to do it right away! They already put the money in escrow. They're waiting for the docs to clear so we can release the merchandise. Yeah, escrow, dummy—no, the account's not linked to us—it's the one I set up in Dee's name. What do you mean you're afraid to do the paperwork? Do I need to come up there and do it for you? Well, if I do, buddy, it's gonna be the last time — because you're as useless as they come." He paused to listen, "Okay, okay, I'll catch a flight out tonight and fix it for you. But, mister, this is the last time I bail you out."

<hr />

As Jared already knew, Steve was doing very well for his business associates. His original business had exported weapons to Iraq and Afghanistan, but soon after 9/11 he quickly extricated his import-export business from the eyes of an extra-vigilant government. Jared also knew that Steve was exporting, among other things, laptop computers to Iran under a legal license. However, what he didn't know what that buried deep within the operating code, if you knew where to find it, was ITAR-sensitive software that wasn't supposed to go to Iran. In fact, although neither party knew it, some of it was secret drone-guidance code that had been developed by Jared's first company. Jared assumed that this was why Stanley considered Steve to be a "person of interest" in the first place.

Several things had happened that Steve wasn't aware of, but Jared was. First, his line of transport was through Qatar to Morocco and then on to Iran. This came to the attention of a Moroccan gentleman who thought he could use Steve's import-export business for his own purposes. He decided to send his daughter Leila, whom he'd produced with his third concubine, to assess Steve and see if this was feasible.

But by then, one of the more intelligent hidden US operatives had intercepted this information and passed the word up the line. His controller called his government friends. The information sat on various desks for the requisite amount of time to enhance each official's importance. Finally, it got to the one person who had the power to give it to Stanley, for a substantial fee, because he knew Stanley had the contacts to make a case. Heads were going to roll over the delay—and they did!

The word was also passed to a lady named Leah, in bed, by one of the minnows in the food chain; Leah then told Stanley's wife what was going on. She then asked her husband to help her friend. Stanley thought it over, weighed the consequences—his fee, his wife's affections, and national security, in that order—and finally talked to Jared over chess and Armagnac. Now the stage was set.

Dee, who overheard parts of Steve's conversation, was one step ahead of him. The king-sized bed with the silk coverlet still held his shaving kit and overnight bag. Once she heard him slam the phone shut she deftly folded what he would need and zipped the bag. He was right behind her; he grabbed it and left without a thank-you. She'd done this before. Steve had abruptly left dinner parties and weekend getaways, always abandoning her to wind things up and make her way home by herself. Slowly she made her way back on deck, just in time to see him slam the gate that led from the dock to the parking lot and run to a waiting taxi.

The wineglass was empty. She thought about opening another bottle and then thought better of it. She wondered where all of Steve's anger came from, but she didn't know enough about his childhood to hazard a guess. She wondered what his father had been like. If he'd had a bad temper, that would have had an effect on Steve. Had he been a rebellious child? Was he punished a lot? She knew enough about child psychology to guess that his anger was deeply rooted. But, how? She might never know, because he never talked about his childhood or his family. It was time to think about what she would do tomorrow: close up the boat by herself again, go back to New York, and then what?

She thought about the locked hatch in the forepeak that Steve had told her not to touch. In his haste he had forgotten it. Determination set in. She opened the second bottle of wine, and then opened the hatch with the bottle opener. Inside was a thick tan briefcase. She picked it up, thinking it was much heavier than she'd expected. She took it to the master stateroom and stared at it for a while, sipping her wine, wondering what was in it, and thinking about what Steve would do to her if she opened it. She decided to slide it under the bunk—unopened for now—and went up onto the bridge deck.

Chapter 4

Later That Evening

THE STATELY KETCH GLIDED IN toward the marina on the evening breeze and rounded up into the wind long enough for the mainsail to be dropped and secured. It was then that Dee noticed there was only one man aboard. She was fascinated as he trimmed the mizzen and jib and headed into the marina. He was going to sail right up to the dock! She watched as he eased the sheets so that the boat lost way and slid gently up to the pier. She couldn't take her eyes off the man as he tied up the ketch and coiled the lines. It wasn't just the lean body that held her attention. She was fascinated by his deftness and his economy of movement. And then there was that face. *Oh my God. His face is handsome as only the sea, the sun, and the wind could make it.*

She stood there watching him, waiting for him to look up at her, as most men did when they saw a pretty woman on the deck of a yacht. But he never did. And once he appeared satisfied with his efforts he disappeared below. She continued to stare at the beautiful wooden sailboat gently swaying in the marina's swells. She noted the name—*Chauffeuse*—and recognized it as the feminine form of the French word *chauffeur*. Men always called their ships and boats "she," but Dee thought that this name was particularly appropriate. This was a vessel to carry a man wherever he wanted to go. After a while she sat down again and picked up her book, but it no longer held her interest. Her mind was busy reliving what she had seen. She'd spent enough time on the water to know that what he had just made look so easy was, in fact, superlative seamanship.

She smiled and found herself fantasizing about him. She wondered if he would be gentle or rough—she'd had enough of rough with Steve, and longed for loving and gentle. But how could you tell by looking at someone? He could even be a hired hand delivering this beautiful sailboat for someone else. She wondered what would be the easiest way to get him to join her for a drink. But then she heard a noise and saw that the man was back on deck with a silver wine bucket. He looked at her and held up two stemmed glasses in invitation. Her breath caught. It took a split second for her to make up her mind. She was up and out of her deck chair, her slender legs skipping down the cruiser's bridge ladder and onto the dock.

The man looked up and watched as she joined him on the ketch. She smiled but her heart raced as she accepted the glass of chilled Chardonnay. Not a word was spoken and less than a minute passed, but she somehow knew her life had just been irrevocably changed. She sipped her wine and waited as the silence lengthened. He didn't seem to want to break it. It was a companionable silence and she began to feel as though she had waited years for him. He looked at her as though he was looking into her entire being. "My name is Jared," he finally said.

Jared's father was the typical self-made man. Educated as an engineer, he founded a small company specializing in state-of-the-art, highly classified, and very expensive military systems whose dubious value was supported only by the politicians waging the Cold War. However, the customers paid on time and in full, so George Herreshoff did not worry about where the systems were being used. As the company's business expanded, George hired a classmate friend, and although he didn't have George's creative engineering talent, he did have the ability to organize and manage people. It was said that Andre could herd cats if it was required to get the job done, shipped, and invoiced. The two got along perfectly and the company grew and prospered. They both married well educated, intelligent women, proficient in the social graces and not unpleasant to gaze upon. George and Alice had two children: Jared and then Alicia; Andre and his wife remained childless.

Both of George and Alice's children proved precocious in the extreme, although predictably, they followed their respective parent's gender proclivities. Alicia was her mother's daughter: tender, loving, and caring, eventually becoming a left-wing Democrat with leanings bordering on socialism. Jared was very much the opposite.

Jared's professional career started at the age of ten. Alice was never satisfied with the landscapers she hired, nor were they with her. Something about her aristocratic air seemed to bring out the mediocrity in them. So, she asked Jared to weed the flower garden behind the house, not wanting the neighbors to see her son working out front at such a menial task. Jared bargained with her and they settled for an extra twenty-five cents on his weekly allowance. After the first week, Jared told his mother that the front of the house needed weeding and for an additional twenty-five cents he would do that too. Alice reluctantly agreed; George watched from a distance and smiled.

Jared then noticed that his neighbor's garden was engorged with weeds and decided that there might be more business there. So he knocked on their door and soon had another customer—at a dollar a week. Flush with his marketing success, he worked the street until he was weeding eight gardens a week. Through word of mouth he was asked to do more. When Alice found out, she was aghast. Her son pulling weeds! She immediately forbade him to do it ever again. He promised compliance, not that it really bothered him because he had tired of pulling weeds several weeks earlier and had hired some of his classmates to work while he raked off 25 percent of the take.

His original twenty-five-cent salary had blossomed to twenty-five dollars a week and he wasn't pulling weeds. With a ready source of labor and the time to do his own quality control, Jared expanded the business. When he was doing the pulling, he was very careful to do a complete job. Now that he had employees—not that a ten-year-old would list them on his income tax return—he had to make sure they did as good a job as he would. After all, the name of his company was "Jared Removes Weeds," so the weeds had better be gone. He learned to enforce discipline and those whose performance was below his standards were first taught, then warned, and finally fired. He was strict, fair, and honest and his classmates/employees appreciated it.

Business was booming when Alice was again apprised of the situation. She was apoplectic! She cornered Jared and George in the living room and confronted them. George had a fit of laughter. How could Jared disobey her and continue pulling weeds in the neighbor's flower gardens? How dare he embarrass her? George was still laughing, which didn't help at all. When she finally ran out of things to say, Jared reminded her that he had only promised not to pull weeds, which he was not doing. Others were doing it for him. He was merely providing jobs and a needed service and managing the whole enterprise. Alice was speechless. She immediately forbade him to do anything remotely related to weeds. George and Jared rolled their eyes at Alice's pronouncement, but she never caught the amused look that passed between them.

Jared finally caved in and told his mother that one of the two boys he had promoted to quality control had mentioned his father had a landscaping company that was struggling, mostly because it had been one of the ones Alice hired and fired. Jared checked them out personally, talked to the father, and convinced one of his customers to try them out. He supervised the trial and when he was satisfied, he negotiated a contract for the company. With this under his belt, he generated a neighborhood monopoly for all of the

21

landscaping business and, with the help of his father, sold his weed-pulling company to the landscaper as part of the deal. Alice couldn't believe it. It got even worse when George recovered sufficiently from laughing to tell her that Jared had made a cool 825 dollars out of her twenty-five cent weeding job. Alice now had visions of dollars and quarters tucked under Jared's mattress, but they assured her that Jared had his own bank account, which would be used for college.

"My little boy," wailed Alice. "My little ten-year-old boy!"

"Actually," said George, "he's eleven. Don't you remember the birthday party you threw for him last month, with all the funny hats and the cake? The friends he invited were his employees!" George then lapsed into another paroxysm of laughter.

"You knew!" screamed Alice, "You knew all along!"

"Yes," said Jared, "he did. And he supported me all along."

Alice looked at Jared with amazed incomprehension; George looked at him with pride.

"Jared? Nice name," Dee said, lamely. *Ouch, this isn't working.* She blushed. But then she heard the music in the background: Brahms. "The second symphony," she said, "in D."

"Very good," replied Jared. "First movement; this section is played by Hermann Baumann on a natural French horn—no valves—so incredibly plaintive."

Dee listened and agreed; it really was beautiful. And from there the conversation blossomed. She found him to be intelligent and cultured. He'd already been apprised of her attributes so it was a pleasant evening. Jared reached over and took her small hand in his, and she felt the warmth of his touch. She looked into his eyes and took in his steady gaze, with just a hint of a smile. He pulled her closer, and she felt his arm come around her—their bodies touching for the first time. She wanted to kiss him, to feel his lips on hers. She felt herself beginning to respond, and thought it had been a very long time since she'd felt the physical pull of passion.

At last he seemed to make up his mind about something, stood up, and headed forward to untie the bow lines and then the stern lines. He was taking the boat out to sea; she knew what was about to happen, and she was ready for it. As they reached the mouth of the inlet, Jared stopped the engine, unfurled the jib, and hoisted mainsail and mizzen. When the wind filled her sails, *Chauffeuse* frolicked in the waves like an eager pup with a bone in her teeth, happy as only a sailboat can be in a good breath of wind.

Dee watched Jared; every line of his body was in concert with the wind and *Chauffeuse*. The smile on his face showed that he was in his element. She fantasized about having a nude painting of him to put in her gallery, but she would never display it. After all, someone might buy it and it would be lost to her forever. She finally understood the people who bought great art that was never seen again. She put down her wineglass and moved to Jared's side. His arm went around her without hesitation, so naturally, so protectively. She felt the power of the wind in the sails, the energy that he was controlling them with a slight movement of his hand and the strength of his body. *Chauffeuse* was loving it; this was what she was made to do, and Jared was the man to sail her. She could feel the power and the joy in him. He looked from the sails to the sea and then down at her. She knew exactly what he was thinking – and her unspoken answer was "Yes!"

Jared brought them to a little cove and anchored. He led her below and took her into his arms. Their first kiss was sweet and tender. He looked down at her and ran his fingers through her hair. She pulled him close to her body and offered herself for a deeper, longer kiss. Then the sense of touch took over and their bodies began to meld together as one. He led her to the stern cabin and began to unbutton her blouse. The rest of their clothes landed on the cabin floor, and he pulled her on top of him on the soft mattress. They could wait no longer for each other. He was long and strong and lean and she was so ready for him that it happened almost too quickly. All she knew was that there was an explosion inside of her that was more powerful than anything she had ever felt in her life. And then they were entwined in each other's arms. She fell into a deep, happy sleep — something so rare for her.

Dee awoke at three bells in the mid-watch. She didn't really know what time it was, but Jared was there so it didn't matter. She was pleased that he was instantly awake, not knowing that real blue-water sailors slept with one eye open. When he returned her middle-of-the-night kiss, she couldn't stop herself.

Okay, it's woman-on-top time! Determined, she shifted position and Jared didn't seem to have a problem. She finally realized at the last moment that he had been watching her and waiting for her. When the orgasm happened, he came deep inside her, and she felt the waves of pleasure over and over again. *Oh my God. He's amazing.* She fell back to sleep in a satisfied haze.

She awoke feeling wonderful and realized it was just before dawn. She lay back to enjoy this new sensation. Jared was no longer next to her. Not bothering to put her clothes on, she went on deck to find him similarly naked. It didn't seem to bother him, so it didn't worry her either. After all, they had just made love, hadn't they? The best sex of her entire life! She came up behind him and hugged him, pressing her naked body against his back. Then she saw Jared scanning the horizon with a pair of binoculars, watching a sport fisherman head out to the Gulf Stream.

She leaned into him affectionately. "Checking the weather?"

Jared said absently, "Steve will be looking for you."

Dee's eyes went wide. She felt like she'd been punched in the stomach. "How do you know about Steve?"

Jared gave her a long look. "Let's say I do know about Steve, but not as much as I need to know. And right now I can't tell you how or why. That will come out in time. It's a homeland security issue."

She crossed her arms over her bare breasts and glared at him. Then she disappeared below and came back wearing shorts and a top; she threw a pair of shorts at Jared.

"What about Steve?" she challenged. "You pull into the slip next to mine, looking like Adonis, and I fall into your arms like a young, infatuated girl. It's obvious you know a lot more about me than I do about you. So, are you going to tell me what's going on?"

Jared winced and looked down at the deck for an inordinate amount of time, given the relative simplicity of her question. "It's a long story," he said, "I'm sorry, but that's all I can tell you right now."

"You're sorry?" echoed Dee. "Well, I'm a whole lot sorrier than you are right now. I have no idea who you are or where you came from. I've fallen into your arms like a lovesick puppy, and I'm confused as hell. And you're sorry? Take me back to the dock, please." Her voice controlled and cold. Jared only nodded and obeyed her wishes. The trip back was silent and as frosty as a voyage to Greenland.

Chapter 5

The Fallout

STEVE HAD TRIED REPEATEDLY TO call Dee the previous evening, but her cell phone must have been turned off. He went through his list of contacts in Miami and came up with one he thought he could trust. Or intimidate. Or buy. He was on the phone with his accountant in a heartbeat.

"If Dee's there, get her ass on a plane back to New York. If not, get Jack down to the marina and pay him whatever he wants. Tell him as soon as Dee shows up to lock the bitch in the big cabin and drive the boat to Nassau. And only pay the bastard half, the rest on delivery. First, you go aboard and get the damned briefcase! The key is under the cushion downstairs up front."

After Dee and Jared had sailed off in *Chauffeuse* the previous evening, Walter—Steve's Miami accountant—gingerly climbed the gangway aboard the *Esmeralda*. He couldn't swim and really didn't like boats of any size. Quite unusual, he often thought, for a man who lives in Miami. He called out for Dee but she didn't answer. That was strange. *Well, maybe she's out shopping.* Still, he was prepared, as always, to follow instructions. As Steve's accountant, he was aware that Dee knew how to spend Steve's money. He headed below to get the briefcase, but when he saw the lock had been forced and the briefcase was gone, he turned white. Heads were going to roll over this one. He didn't even look for it, but ran back on deck to call Steve and then make plans to be in a remote place until Steve calmed down.

26

Dee stomped off *Chauffeuse* with as much anger, indignation, and frustration as a barefoot woman could muster and headed back to *Esmeralda*. Who was Jared? How did he know about Steve? How much did he know about her? Did he already understand what was happening in her marriage? Why was he here? Then she realized that he had to be here for a reason. But what? And who sent him?

She poured another glass of tea and realized it was only 8:30 a.m. She was disgusted with herself; she was hurt, frustrated, and humiliated... not to mention tired. She went below to the master stateroom to think some more. Within minutes her thoughts transformed themselves into gentle snores.

Jared had watched Dee leave and then went below without even washing down *Chauffeuse*, a task he seldom neglected. She was his pride and joy. He got out his old meerschaum pipe with the face of a ship's captain carved onto the bowl, came back on deck and filled it with Mac Baren's Latakia Blend. The morning was clear and bright as he tried to put the puzzle together in his mind. But after a few puffs, fatigue took over and he went below.

That turned out to be a mistake.

Dee awoke suddenly when she heard the diesels starting. She ran to the cabin door only to find it had been locked from the outside. This was totally against Coast Guard regulations, unless it was intended as a prison cell. She banged her fists on it and then got on the intercom.

"What's going on? Let me out of here!"

"Sorry, lady," a male voice answered. "I've got orders to get

27

this boat to Nassau with you aboard. You'll find coffee and a cold lunch on the counter and the head still works, so sit back and enjoy the ride. I'll unlock your cabin door."

Dee was aghast. Could this be Jared's doing? No, of course not. Even in the short time she had known him she could not believe that. Steve? Oh, yes! He would do something like this. Damn him!

And Jared, the one person she wanted the most now, needed the most now, was gone.

Chapter 6

Dee's Rescue

J ARED WAS SUDDENLY WIDE AWAKE. He lay there for several moments analyzing what had changed. A motor, no two, had started—that meant someone was leaving the marina. He checked his watch; it was 10:30 a.m. Could it be a fishing boat? No, not here. Not with two very powerful engines and not this late in the morning. He slipped out of his bunk noiselessly and headed on deck.

The *Esmeralda* was easing away from the dock—with Dee aboard! She didn't know how to start the engines, much less take the boat out to sea. The sudden realization that she was likely being kidnapped hit Jared and his heart raced.

It took him a moment to recognize who must be at the wheel. It had to be Jack Cochran, the only person in all of South Florida who could be persuaded to take on a kidnapping. Jared knew Jack by reputation. Jack had lost his master's papers over a year ago and had been working as a mate whenever he could find someone willing to overlook that minor requirement. What the hell was he doing on the *Esmeralda*? Worse yet, where was he taking Dee?

Jared bellowed in a voice that would raise the watch below. "Jack, I know that's you! Where are you taking that boat?"

The only response from the bridge was a hand signal with an upraised middle digit. Then the throttles advanced and the *Esmeralda* accelerated down the channel, soon to be lost in trailing gray diesel exhaust. He was angry at himself. He should have known Steve would try something like this. If only he had kept Dee with him.

If only they hadn't argued, he thought. If only, if only!

All right, he thought to himself, *trim the sails and let's get underway.* Realizing he couldn't catch Jack with the *Chauffeuse*, he knew he needed another plan. Where would Jack go? The Keys? Not with a fifty-four-foot Bertram. Too obvious. Jared wondered whether Steve had ordered Jack to get the *Esmeralda* out of the country for some reason. If so, where to? The Bahamas? Nassau? Freeport? Of course! Freeport would be an easy trip, but Nassau was Jack's old fishing grounds. Jared recalled there was a deepwater marina in Nassau named Yacht Haven, where Jack could leave it; it wouldn't even be noticed among the other yachts. And there was an international airport there, which would come in handy if Steve wanted to fly Dee back to New York. Besides, Steve was into flashy—and that spelled Paradise Island. *I'm rolling the dice on one of two odds, and I'd better be right.*

But Jared had to get there before Jack could fly Dee out. A quick check showed him there weren't any commercial flights or charter flights available. So he called in a marker with an old friend who owned a Cigarette boat. Although the man wasn't happy about being awakened and unceremoniously dragged from the arms of his latest nubile lass, Jared did manage to persuade him to join the chase. Before they got too far out to sea, Jared was already on his cell phone making plans.

It was a molar-grinding, kidney-bashing, spine-crushing hell-on-water, 160-mile ride across the Gulf Stream—but Jared was almost positive they had arrived before Dee. The rest was easy. He had contacts on Paradise Island who were more than willing to watch for the *Esmeralda* and to call him when Jack arrived with info about his destination. And Jared set them up with drinks at three of the bars there, with massive remunerations for the staff to keep their mouths shut. If he was wrong and Dee was in Freeport, then, of course, he would have a real problem. The thought of failure made his blood run cold.

Jared's cell phone rang. "Got him, chief. He just arrived at Yacht Haven. Imagine he'll be at the bar in the Poop Deck as soon as he clears customs."

It didn't take long until Jack swaggered in, looking full of himself, and took a seat at the bar. "Rum," he said, "and make it a double!"

"There's one in front of you," said the bartender, "compliments of that gentleman over there." Jack looked to his left but the seat was empty. Then a hand came down hard on his shoulder. A hand calloused from hauling sheets and halyards on a sailing vessel.

"We need to talk," said Jared.

Jack considered his options. He knew whose hand was on his shoulder: a hand that shouldn't be there because it should be back in Miami, a hand that wouldn't be there if the man who owned it hadn't been very determined to be in this bar before Jack got there. He knew his options were limited and that Jared was not a happy man. And, he knew there was physical pain down that road. So he took the best option he had—gulped down his rum and hung his head.

"What do you want to know?" The hand relaxed its grip slightly.

"Where's Dee?"

"On the *Esmeralda*. And she's as comfortable as can be expected. The accountant told me if anything happened to her, I'd be shark bait."

"I know that. Where?"

"Master stateroom. I locked her up and left the keys in the

galley. Look, Jared, it was a job for me. I was short of cash and this accountant-type guy showed up and offered me a wad to bring the *Esmeralda* here and keep Dee on board until they could pick her up in the morning and fly her back to her husband."

"Who's they? Why didn't they grab her in Miami?"

"I don't know, but I'll back you if you'll get me out of this."

"Somehow, Jack, I don't think I want you behind me. Take whatever you've got and get out of here."

Jack reconsidered his options. Perhaps he could contact the accountant and warn him about Jared. The hand on his shoulder tightened again. Maybe that wasn't such a good idea. If he did, Jared would hunt him down personally and that wouldn't be pleasant.

"Jared," he lied, "they haven't paid me yet. I need something to get me out of here."

Jared reached in his shirt pocket, and pulled out a wad of bills, and stuffed it down Jack's shirt. "I don't ever want to see your face again." He slowly turned him around and looked into his eyes. Jack never wanted to look into those eyes again, either.

"I'm gone," he said, and scuttled sideways out of the bar.

———

Jared walked down the pier to the *Esmeralda*, deep in thought. Why did Steve want the boat here? How did he know that Dee wasn't on board the *Esmeralda* last night? Why not snatch Dee in Miami, take her home and spank her there? Why Jack and the accountant? Who was coming to get Dee? Hmmm… He found himself next to the companionway and, without hesitation, boarded the *Esmeralda*—he was pretty sure he would own her soon, anyway. Not that he liked the smell of diesel smoke or the throb of engines when the wind was fresh, but he had a premonition that he would acquire her from Steve and sell her for half her worth just to cleanse her of the memories she carried deep in her hull. Dee was safe below, and he needed to think, so he went to the bridge, sat in the captain's chair, put his feet up on the console, and did just that. He wished he had his pipe; it always calmed him down and seemed to clear his mind.

It didn't take long after the adrenaline drained from his system for him to flex his tired muscles, relax, and finally nap. When he awoke an hour later, the pieces of the puzzle rearranged themselves in his mind, merged with everything else he knew about Steve, and rearranged themselves again. Two calls on his cell phone verified his analysis. Okay, that was the cerebral part, but now it was already evening, and he still had to contend with whoever "they" were who were coming for Dee and the other valuable thing that Steve wanted back from the *Esmeralda*. One of his calls verified that the boat was mortgaged to the hilt, so leaving her here would make repossession difficult. He smiled and decided he didn't want to acquire her at all. Let Steve contend with the legal costs and the hassle that came with that.

Jared was about to go below and wake Dee when he felt a subtle change in the motion of the boat. Someone had come aboard; no, there were two of them. Damn, he didn't think they would be here this soon. He quietly looked around for a weapon but all he could find was a billy club. Oh well, if there were only two of them, the billy should do. That and surprise: Dee still didn't know he was here, so she couldn't give him away. He peered cautiously over the coaming and saw them head below. He slid silently down to the cockpit and patiently waited beside the companionway hatch, until he heard voices. More correctly, Dee's voice in an allegro molto fortissimo of demands and threats. The male voices were silent in this chorus.

Dee heard them first: the sound of keys unlocking several doors before they unlocked hers. Steve's thugs had come for her and she was not a happy camper. "Damned accountant might have told us the keys were in the kitchen," she heard one say. She thought to herself: *Galley, you jerk, it's a galley on a boat, not a kitchen. Well, they certainly aren't sailors.* Then the door opened and they were there. The larger of the two grabbed a suitcase and threw it on the bed. "Pack," he said, "You're going to New York. And where's the damn briefcase?"

"Go to hell!" she hissed at him.

The smaller of the two grabbed her arm and brought it up behind her back.

"Go to hell, you creeps!" she spat again.

"Never mind," said Larger, "It's here under the bed." Smaller pushed Dee's arm up just a little farther to give her a taste of what might happen. "Bastard," she said.

Smaller threw whatever clothes were at hand into the suitcase and slammed it shut. "Let's get off this floating circus," he said.

Jared watched as Dee was escorted unceremoniously onto the deck and waited until both men were visible. One had Dee by the arm and held a black suitcase in the other hand.

Very unprofessional, thought Jared. *If you want to do what you do for a living, you always need to keep one hand free.* Perhaps Jared might have said "Unhand the damsel" and stood in battle with them, but the odds were two to one, and Jared hadn't made his fortune by being kind to his enemies. Without warning he used the billy club to break the forearm of the one closest to him and hit him in the chest with it. Smaller let go of the suitcase and somersaulted back down the companionway, where the subsequent proceedings interested him no longer.

That left Larger, who was holding on to Dee with one hand and grasping the bulky tan briefcase with the other. His obvious moment of indecision sealed his fate. Jared came at him with the club just as Dee drove her spike heel deep into his instep. He was about to let out a bellow of surprise and anguish when Jared tapped him on the head with the club and helped him join his silent partner. Dee slipped her foot out of the sandal and bent down to pull it out of her assailant. She looked at it with disgust and threw it over the rail. Then she took off the other sandal and threw that over the rail, too. Finally, she looked at Jared.

"What took you so long to get here?"

"I needed a nap," said Jared. "It was a long day."

"Tell me about it!" And then she grabbed him and kissed him.

"What now?" she said opening the suitcase and extracting a new pair of stiletto sandals.

"Those really wreck these beautiful teak decks," said Jared, taking the suitcase and handing her the briefcase, "but I'm glad you wore them today."

"I do it to make Steve angry, but he doesn't care; this boat's just another thing to him." She hesitated and added, "Just like me."

Jared turned her to face him and looked deep into her eyes. She had seen that look before, but now there was something different about it. He looked as though there was something he was trying to find, some place he hadn't visited in a very long time, some decision he couldn't quite make. He turned away from her and said, "It's time we disappeared."

She gave him a long look and followed him down the pier.

The car at the entrance was parked in a tow-away zone with the keys in it and Jared reckoned that it belonged to the sleeping escorts. Dee looked at Jared inquisitively, but Jared shook his head. He was on the phone as they walked. After a while he said, "I have reservations at a local hotel. Would you prefer your own room or will you share mine?"

"I'll feel safer with you," Dee said quickly. "But I'll sleep on the other bed if you don't mind."

Then she asked, "Who were you talking to?"

"Melanie. She works for me. She's made reservations for us under assumed names and is taking care of the clowns who were trying to abduct you."

"What are our new names?"

"Alicia and Jared Wheaton."

"Who?"

"She's also getting us a flight out of here tomorrow morning."

"Give me your phone," said Dee, while diving into her purse. She apparently found what she was looking for, and a few minutes later said, "I thought Steve would use the same charter service. There's a plane waiting for us now; I thought that could happen, since Steve was planning to kidnap me, and I guess he doesn't know yet that you foiled his plot. He sent the plane here to pick me up once Captain Jack brought me here. But now it's too late to get clearance for New York. I told them to lay over until 8 a.m. Is that all right?"

Jared looked at her and gave her an impulsive hug. "You mean Steve is paying for our flight home?"

"Yes, damn him! And it's under my name."

Jared shook his head and laughed. What had Stanley gotten him into? And what a woman Dee was turning out to be! He took his phone back, and later when Dee was in the bathroom, he called Melanie and told her he didn't need the corporate jet sent down to pick them up.

Dee and Jared sat in a quiet bistro on Paradise Island. The food and wine were excellent and they talked of her life with Steve and why she had married him.

"Jared, I know it's not much of an excuse, but I was tired. I loved my best clients and they loved me. I appreciated their enthusiasm for the artwork I found for them. I guess I wished I could share their lifestyle. But I was tired of the rest of it, tired of being on my feet all day, tired of working for peanuts, and tired of working such long hours that I had no time for a life. I was lonely and wanted the same kind of life my clients had. It was within reach, but at the same time, it wasn't. I was there, but I wasn't there either. I was about ready to give up and go home—home to my little town, to the only life I'd known. I was sad that my dream of living in New York didn't measure up. It meant, in essence, that I didn't measure up. I saw Steve as my way out."

She sighed and sat back, staring into space, thoughtful. Jared saw relief on her face and wondered if she'd ever vocalized her thoughts this way before. He somehow doubted it.

When they returned to their room and readied themselves for sleep, Jared got into bed and found he had a bedmate. He held her tight and remarked about it.

"Go to sleep," was the reply as Dee snuggled into his shoulder.

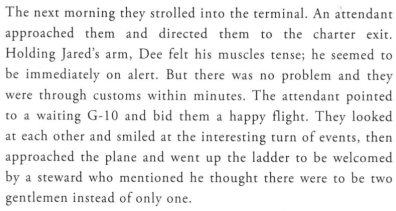

The next morning they strolled into the terminal. An attendant approached them and directed them to the charter exit. Holding Jared's arm, Dee felt his muscles tense; he seemed to be immediately on alert. But there was no problem and they were through customs within minutes. The attendant pointed to a waiting G-10 and bid them a happy flight. They looked at each other and smiled at the interesting turn of events, then approached the plane and went up the ladder to be welcomed by a steward who mentioned he thought there were to be two gentlemen instead of only one.

"I dismissed him," said Dee with disdain. "He was rude. Now, it's early and I'm hungry – and as soon as we're airborne we'd like Bloody Marys and breakfast."

"Of course, madam" came the only possible response.

"And please inform the flight crew that there's been a change of destination. Have them file a plan for… " Here Dee hesitated and Jared filled in, "Washington, DC."

"Of course, madam." The pilot excused himself and headed forward. Dee and Jared were beside themselves with the absurdity of it all. They were flying home in a charter jet Steve had paid for. They waited patiently until the plane lifted off and the Marys were served to touch glasses and really laugh.

Dee loved the feel of the jet's powerful engines; she stared out the window to the glittering blue of the shallow ocean surrounding the Bahamas. "There's no blue like it anywhere in the world," she told Jared. "And it's especially beautiful today."

Their initial laughter subsided and they looked at each other. Jared reached for the tan briefcase but she put her hand on his. "We need to talk," she said. "Tell me how you know about Steve. But first, tell me who you are."

"I'm Jared Herreshoff. Distantly related to the great yacht designer."

"So whose sailboat were you delivering to Miami?" she said, knowing the answer but afraid of it.

"*Chauffeuse* is mine," he answered.

She knew the value of fine works of art and she could only guess at the time, effort and expense it took to keep the wooden ketch in such pristine condition.

"I brought her down from Ft Lauderdale to Miami to be here with you."

"By yourself?"

"Easy sail. I gave the crew a two-month vacation because next year we have the Marion to Bermuda Race to contend with. This year she finished third in her class in the Newport to Bermuda. We hope to do better in the next one."

Dee watched him closely and saw the boyish pleasure in his eyes; what she saw there was a deep-rooted enjoyment of the purity of the wind and the sea and sailing that brought to mind the purity of innocent love that she had been longing for.

She took a deep breath, searching for the right way to phrase her next question. The best she could do was, "I'm lost. Tell me about yourself. How did you get where you are today?"

"I am not impoverished," he said. "In fact, I am really quite well off. I am semi-retired, so I enjoy life and choose only the adventures that intrigue me. After college I was hired by a start-up company that developed state-of-the-art commercial autopilots for the marine industry. I worked my way up to president and when we sold out and went public, I became a very wealthy man. So here I am."

"Self-made too," she chuckled. "I like that."

"You don't know the half of it! I started, ran, and sold my first business when I was ten. Now that's a story to tell you about when we have some time. It was one of the highlights of my youth. I don't know how many times my father told that story to his business friends. He was so damned proud of me!"

What Jared didn't tell her was that when he went to the local public high school, he was an instant success. Since he was good looking, of above average height, with a ready smile, he did not have any trouble making friends. It became obvious to all from the beginning that Jared did not choose his friends on any pejorative assumptions, but rather on his individual assessment. If he found in them common bonds with his own, they were his friends; if not he ignored them. "Life is too short to waste it with fools," was his favorite saying. He got excellent grades with ease. He joined the debating club and in his first debate he demolished his senior class opponent. The subject was, "The benefits of the progressive income tax system." Since he had run his own business at the age of ten, he took the opposing side.

Jared went out for sports, both swimming and track, preferring them because he could contribute as an individual to the team's success or failure. He probably would have graduated first or second in his class if it were not for the professor who was proctor for the debating club. This man had taken an instant dislike to him because of the first debate when Jared was a freshman. In what was a more or less subjective course, he found many ways to penalize Jared for his conservative thoughts, awarding a B plus for the semester. The professor smiled derisively when he personally told Jared about the grade.

Jared just looked into his eyes and smiled, "You have taught me much more than you realize." They both knew what that meant.

So he graduated third in his class, poorer by accolade but wiser by far.

His college selection was a free-for-all. His mother had secretly applied for pre-admittance to Harvard for him and it was duly granted. She had several friends with influence to assure this, one of whom had invited an indiscreet liaison in the past, to which she had complied, calculating that it might be a trump to be played in the future. It took the trick. Unbeknownst to her, Dad had called his old buddies to get Jared into MIT—with equal success. He was very proud of himself. Mother doubled down her bet and did the same thing with her Wellesley classmates to get him into Brandeis. Dad thought about it for a while, made some calls, and was assured that Jared would also be welcome at Boston College.

The revelation of these machinations at home had to be attended to be believed. Ranting and raving were rampant on a field of dire imprecations. Mother and Dad were adamant in their belief that each had the right to decide. So Jared waited until the two ran out of breath, and then informed them of his acceptance, with a scholarship, to Worcester Polytechnic and that was where he would get his engineering education. Period. End of discussion. He got up, hugged his speechless mother and father, and left the room.

When he got to WPI he was six foot three, with a body hardened by swimming and track. There was a lean and hungry look in his eyes, which could be merry or flint hard, for behind them were the experiences of his high school career, some good, some bad, but all a part of him now. As before, he was accepted socially by both his classmates and the upperclassmen, who recognized him as a born leader. He was rushed by all of the fraternities on campus and accepted the invitation to TKE, and after the requisite hazing (which he took with good grace) he was duly initiated as a brother. As it turned out, he had fulfilled his father's predictions for his success in high school. In fact, he wound up tutoring some of his classmates who hadn't had the benefit of his education, which got them through the tough first semester. This extracurricular activity also did not go unnoticed by the upperclassmen.

One required course amused him the most. He had to participate in the Reserve Officers Training Course. It was designed to provide basic training for men who might, at some future time, be required to serve as officers in the Army. He rather enjoyed the parading, learning to march in time, formation drill, polishing his shoes to a mirror-like shine and all of the other fun things that went with such an exercise. But then came the day when the sergeant took his platoon to the rifle range. The object was to teach the students to shoot accurately at a target, or at least not to endanger each other. Jared's first five shots were so tightly grouped that the sergeant thought he had only hit the target three times and had missed the whole thing twice. Jared repeated the drill, but this time spaced the shots around the center so that they could be identified, but each touched the ten ring to give him a perfect score of fifty. The sergeant shook his head, incredulous. Jared had learned to shoot when he was ten, taught by his father, who was serious about accuracy and gun safety. George's maxim was, "If you shoot it, then you have to eat it!" They hunted deer every fall and Jared learned to cook venison in gourmet variations, something his mother and sister abhorred. However, Jared never had to baste one of his hunting companions.

Although his father was an electrical engineer, Jared chose mechanical engineering as his major. He was fascinated by machinery and the elegance of fine cars, clever mechanisms, and the design of devices to produce products faster, easier, reliably, and more profitably. As a result, his grades were again exemplary. Because the school thought he should have some familiarity with the humanities, he was required to take courses in liberal arts, which he did with his usual attention and excellence. What really intrigued him was an elective course in philosophy, so much so that he asked the professor for extra reading material, guaranteeing himself an easy "A" here too, but when he started spending extra time discussing what he had read, the professor realized that Jared was really interested, although he could not see why at first.

Four years later Jared graduated first in his class by a narrow margin. His valedictory address focused not on what he owed to the world with his newly found knowledge, but on what he himself could do with it, by himself, for himself, and if he did that well, then and only then would others benefit. Amazingly, he got a standing ovation for such a radical speech and this quite amazed him. Not that he cared all that much, for he had already set his sight on a new goal: his first job as an engineer in the real world. Now he could see for himself if he was really good at it. He was.

"How old are you?" Dee asked.

"Three years your senior," said Jared.

"All right! I've had enough! How do you know that? Who put you up to this?" she exploded.

"It's okay," he said, giving her a little hug to reassure her. "I'll tell you the whole story. Someone called a friend, who called a friend, and so on, and I wound up at the pointy end of the spear.

The exact wording went like this: 'Jared, my friend, you might be the perfect person help me in a somewhat contiguous but unrelated problem. My wife has a friend whose sister is married to a 'person of interest.' The request came back up the food chain and I, unfortunately, happened to be the chef du jour. Now I am supposed to find the truth, exculpate the husband or extricate the sister, all without disturbing the status quo and without anyone knowing that I am at all involved. That is, without any official intercession. Can you help?' I was intrigued, so I looked into it."

"This is what you do when you're not winning yacht races?" Dee asked, still visibly flustered. "Wait a minute! My sister Leah?"

"The very same. Now, let's get down to business. What I do now for fun is to find start-ups that have a great idea but are a little challenged in business acumen. Then I buy in, bring some of my network in, and make it happen for them. Everyone becomes very rich and so far, in the last six years, if I may humbly say, I've had an impressive success rate of 85 percent. So when my friend Stanley proposed that I look into a personal problem, I was, as I said, intrigued."

Dee nodded, and Jared could see that she was paying close attention.

"When I go into ventures, I try to find two critical things. One is the fulcrum on which the whole enterprise is balanced: success on one side and failure on the other. The second is finding the answer to tip that balance toward success. With you and Steve, I already know the major point and the major question. The point is that Steve is in way over his head. I'm not sure there is a way to get him out of the cesspool he's in. I shall try, although it's not something I really want to do. The question is whether you want to be extricated or go down with this clown."

Jared watched as her eyes widened and her mouth opened as she tried to take in everything he was telling her.

43

"Get me out of this—" she started to say, but then collapsed back into her seat. "It won't work. Steve will come after us; he's a maniac about his possessions. And I'm one of them. He'll find ways to hurt you and me that you can't imagine." Tears started in her eyes. "Please don't."

Jared gently took her hand. "Yes, I know that about him, but so far he's not doing very well. He's only had me to contend with and we are now flying in his jet while his hired thugs nurse their wounds and explain themselves to the Nassau authorities. By the way, I made a call to a friend I have among those authorities who will make them very uncomfortable, indeed. And their car has been towed. Did I mention I have a network of friends whom I have made very happy, not only monetarily, but with the thrill of the chase? They are going to love this."

Dee looked at him dubiously. Then a glimmer of hope spread across her face. She looked in his eyes again and that vanished. "Get me out of this." This time she whispered it.

And Jared suddenly realized that for the first time in years he felt protective of a woman. He wasn't ready to admit it, but deep down he knew—he was falling for Dee.

"First, I'll get you somewhere that Steve will never think to look," said Jared.

"Where?"

"My mother's townhouse in Georgetown."

"What then?"

"I already know where he's vulnerable," said Jared, "but let's see what's in here." And again he reached for the briefcase, but it was locked. Jared stared at the lock and wondered where he had seen one like it before. Then he remembered it was a courier case and, if forced, the contents could be destroyed. Melanie used this type of case in the side business she ran carrying sensitive documents. She also knew someone who could open them if necessary. Jared smiled, knowing that getting Melanie to work for him had been one of his best investments.

"Now tell me about yourself."

Chapter 7

Dee's Story

DEE THOUGHT FOR A MINUTE and then began to talk, slowly at first, and then the words began to flow. "I guess you could say I was a small-town girl with big-city ideas. I did all the normal things girls do, from playing on the swings in the local park, to riding bicycles out in the country, to flirting with boys, and going to football games with friends to cheer for our team. We had a central school district, so friends came from all around the area. Our parents were too busy working to drive us places, so we rode our bikes for three seasons and then settled in for the snowy winter. Then we would ski and ice skate and, if we were lucky, someone made a bonfire on Saturday nights."

She stopped to gauge Jared's reaction; he smiled and nodded his head, as if her words were somehow giving him back a few memories of his own. When she stopped he looked over and asked, "And were you the prettiest and most popular girl in school, Dee?"

"Oh, no, not even close! I was awkward—all arms and legs until about the age of twelve or thirteen. Then I started to fill out, in what I guess were all the right places. At least the boys seemed to think so. But my mom and dad kept a close eye on me because they were afraid I'd become boy crazy. So I did my homework, always with an eye on ways to get out of the house to meet my friends. There were always two sides to me: the side that knew what was expected of me, and the side that just wanted to get out and have fun."

"And did you?" Jared asked.

"I had enough, I guess. Enough to know that as soon as I could get away from home and my parents' eagle eyes, the sooner I would have a life of my own. That's why I studied: so I could go to college. My goal was to live in New York City. I'd read all the magazines about the big city, and I knew that's where I wanted to be. I knew I would have to make some sacrifices to have that life, although I didn't have the crystal ball that would tell me the things I really needed to know, like how tiny the apartments were, how fast the money went, how noisy a city could be—even at four in the morning when the delivery trucks and the garbage trucks came down your block."

Jared nodded. "Dreams versus reality. In our dreams all we see are the good parts. If our brains were able to see everything, maybe we wouldn't want to follow those dreams." Jared sighed. "And wouldn't that be sad?"

"Oh, and I have a little sister. Her name is Leah, but we call her 'Lee.'" She stopped. "Oh, but you know that already, don't you? What else do you know?"

He hesitated as if holding back. The second's hesitation was enough for Dee.

"So you know a lot about me already," she said quietly, and then sat still for a minute, lost in thought. She was completely out of her comfort zone. This was not a place she'd ever been before. Oh, sure, she'd flown on private jets, but never with someone who could see her from the inside out like Jared.

He said quietly, "I know a few facts. Enough to know that you did get your wish to be a big-city girl. Tell me about that. I want to know if your dream became a reality."

"Before we get there, though, I need to tell you something about my very early life, and how my life changed in the blink of

46

an eye. If I don't tell you that story, the rest might not even make sense. You see, Jared, there is a part of me that I have buried so deeply, so carefully, that I have to dig it out to get it back. But it's at the heart of who I am, so let me tell you, okay?"

Jared nodded, showing that he was giving her his full attention.

———————

At the age of three, I was the princess in my little world of Grandmother and Grandfather—and that included the house, the barn, the outbuildings, the gardens, the fields, and the animals – oh yes, definitely all of the animals. I was there, big as life, and holding court, when the cows were milked, when the eggs were collected, and when the dogs and cats were fed. I roamed the farm as though I owned it. It was not a wealthy farm, as farms go, but it had everything I could ever want, including my grandparents, who doted on me. No, let's be honest, they spoiled me rotten, and I would have been called a brat were it not for the intense love the three of us had for each other. You see, I was the first grandchild, and my mother, Evelyn, was gone more than she was home. She had made a career of being an officer's wife, and it was so much easier to leave me behind and play the social climber without me.

So, at an early age I could already sing children's songs along with my grandfather's piano playing, weed the rows of tiny carrots that Grandma planted, and steal the warm brown eggs out from under the clucking hens. I used to carry around my favorite basket, filling it with treats from the garden: peas to shuck, ripe tomatoes, and small bunches of grapes, or even apples that had dropped from the neighbor's trees.

I wasn't merely precocious; in some ways I was a tiny adult, having been included in my grandma's conversations ever since I was in my high chair. Grandma would pour herself a cup of coffee, and then carefully prepare a second cup for me: a teaspoon of coffee in a cup of milk, carefully stirred with some sugar or honey. Then we would have a chat. It didn't matter what we were talking about; rather, it was the fact that we were talking that counted, especially when neighbors were a mile down the road and working on their own farms during the day.

Grandma would begin: "What do you think of Ruth and Dan's new brown calf?" I would answer, "I was hoping for a girl, but they named this one Buster, so he must be a boy. I think he's cute, but I do want to go back to play with the kittens in the barn. Can we keep the white one, Grandma? Can we please?" Grandma would consider my request very seriously and then tell me that maybe that was a good idea, considering all the mice we had in the barn. And then I would tell my grandma that she was the best grandma in the whole wide world.

And so the years when I was two, and then three, went along peacefully, changing with the seasons, the quiet winters when we ate the canned goods and read to each other, the busy spring full of planting and new births, the wonderful hot summers and the glorious harvest season. I thrived in the simple life, basking in the love of my grandparents, and becoming very sure of myself. I was smart and cocky, with a vocabulary that startled the neighbors, and there was never a hint of baby talk in my long chats with them.

Then the bottom fell out. My mother showed up at the farm one afternoon in late spring and announced that we were moving to a new home, away from my grandparents' farm. My father had left the military and had taken a civilian position that would give us a good living, but it required that we move. My father, who I had barely seen through the years, had already found us a place to live and was preparing it for our arrival. It was in a town only forty-five miles from the farm, but for me, it might as well have been a thousand! I had two days to say good-bye to my grandparents and the only life I had ever known. You see, Jared, my parents were practically strangers to me.

Through the thin walls of the new house Dee heard her mother retching in the bathroom in the early morning. It didn't take Dee long to observe her mother's growing belly and equate it with the farm animals and the young they brought forth. She knew her days of being an only child were almost over. She missed her grandmother with an almost physical pain. She was already too old to bond with this stranger who called herself Mother. Dee missed the freedom of roaming the farm and the fields, and she hated the constraints of life in the suburbs. At night she fell asleep dreaming of running in green meadows and playing with the baby lambs.

And then, with a flurry of activity, she was being readied for kindergarten. There was a shopping trip to buy Dee new clothes. Gone were the little flowered dresses and shorts that Grandma made her, replaced by serious plaid skirts and white blouses and her first pair of black shoes. She was provided with boxes of pencils and crayons, pads of paper, and even a little satchel to carry it all in. For Dee, this was the first good thing that had happened to her since she'd been taken from her grandparents' farm.

A very pregnant Evelyn walked Dee to school that first day and met her teacher. Dee didn't mind that it was called kindergarten— she was in school. She already knew her letters and numbers, and was almost reading, so she was able to enjoy being part of this new adventure, which she adored from the start. She especially loved to draw with her new crayons, and she took very good care not to break any. She valued all of her belongings with a passion. This teacher, as with many in years to come, would take note of Dee and remark on the child's beauty and intelligence. But what they noticed most of all was a kind of wistfulness that Dee would exhibit at times, as if she were physically there, but her mind was far away.

By Christmas, Dee was a big sister. Her parents named the baby Leonora, which Dee promptly shortened to Leah. Dee had never been near an infant before, and she was fascinated by this baby's every move, and fascinated beyond belief as the baby grew and *developed a personality all her own. So there began a new rhythm in Dee's life. She would go to school, where she worked hard, and then race home to take care of the baby. Mother once again showed signs of distancing herself from her offspring and let Dee take on more of the Leah's care as the months and then the years passed.*

Eventually Dee and Leah came to an understanding: Dee was the de facto mother, and their biological mother was something of a stranger to them both. As Leah noted many years later, "We didn't bond with our mother; we bonded with each other." Although there was almost six years between them, Dee and Leah were friends and were happy together, with Dee always taking the role of mother or teacher. And so the years passed peacefully, as the two sisters grew and flourished. Evelyn, however, did not. She suffered from bouts of depression, often closing herself in a dark bedroom for days at a time.

All this time, Dee's dad, the ex-Major William Wheaton, was trying to earn a living. He was a virtual stranger to his daughters, and treated his wife with indifference, given her so-called ailment. Sometimes he would make a good sale to a foreign buyer and come home with a new car, or at other times he would tell them all to "make do, because times are tight." He never discussed his business with anyone, and the only indication of whether times were good or bad was the hour he arrived home and the size of the whiskey he'd pour for himself. Once in a while he would disappear for days and come home after one of his business trips looking like "something the cat dragged in." Evelyn would tell him as much and then disappear into her room again. Dee and Leah learned to fend for themselves. By the time she was twelve, and Leah six, Dee could put together a decent meal, do the laundry and ironing, and keep the house neat.

When she was seventeen, Dee learned to drive a car and purchased her own with babysitting money. She had, within the limits of living at home, the freedom to roam and to enjoy time with her friends. But her days of living in a small town had come to an end. Her high school diploma, and her good grades, earned her a place in one of the better liberal arts colleges in her dream city—New York. She hugged Leah until they both cried, and then she boarded the train that would take her down the Hudson River to her new life.

Chapter 8

Washington, DC

J ARED AND DEE THANKED THE crew when they landed at Reagan International, which was more than Steve and his cohorts ever did after a flight. A taxi whisked them to Jared's mother's townhouse in a quiet Georgetown neighborhood. The peace and serenity was the result of a groundswell of wealth, and it was not lost on Dee. Jared paid the driver and raced up the steps, punched in the security code, apparently from memory, and escorted her into the foyer. Their arrival was silently announced by the system and the door was opened by the largest man she had ever seen. Immaculately dressed in a tuxedo that must have taken five yards of cloth to tailor, he filled the doorway from side to side and up to the lintel.

"Jared! How good to see you again," he said in a voice so deep that it seemed to emanate from his ankles. "Your mother is eagerly waiting for you. And this beautiful lady is, I assume, Dee?"

"Yes, indeed. Dee, may I present to you Samuel? He and his wife reside here and are companions for my mother. Samuel is working on his PhD in Polynesian History, and Clarissa, whom you will soon meet, has her degree in culinary arts. Wait until you taste her food—it's amazing."

Dee wondered how many truckloads of food Clarissa had to cook each day to fill her huge husband, and then stifled a giggle when she imagined the size of the woman to match this man. The giggle almost escaped when she thought of further implications.

Samuel ushered them into the sitting room and formally

announced them. Both he and Jared had twinkles in their eyes. Alice looked up from her novel, peered at Jared and Dee, and rose to greet Dee with a hug. As she pulled back, she looked deep into Dee's eyes and stood there for a moment, as if taking her in. Although visibly tired, Dee carried herself like a lady, and Alice's smile indicated her appreciation. Dee was reluctant to end the embrace, and suddenly found herself wondering what it would be like to hug her own mother, who would now, like Alice, also be in her late sixties.

"Dee," said Alice, carefully spooning sugar into her tea. The two of them were seated in Alice's perfectly decorated sunroom. "Dee, now what kind of a name is that?" she asked.

Dee didn't even notice that Samuel and Jared had quietly retired, leaving her alone with Alice.

"Actually, my name is Dorothy—Dorothy Barbara, after my two grandmothers—but that was too much for me when I was little, so it became Dee, and it's been that way ever since."

Alice watched as Dee sipped her black coffee and set it down carefully on the rattan side table. She kept observing her, but Dee was cautious and guarded; she barely smiled, and, although she was tired, she tried to sit up straight and to look Alice in the eye.

"You know, my dear, Jared has not brought anyone home to Mother since his college days, and that's been quite a long time."

Dee's eyes widened, and she answered.

"I am sure the circumstances were probably different then, too. He most likely brought some pretty college girl home for the weekend?"

"Yes, my dear, that's how it was. Pretty little thing she was, too. He brought her just that one time and never again. She stayed with us for two weeks. I was living in a different house at the time, of course—Jared bought this place for me when George died—but they seemed to be so in love with each other.

53

He was studying that engineering thing that he does and she was studying... wait I have to think... biomedical something or other. They would talk for hours and I never understood a word they said. But they would sit at the table with classical music in the background and our fat chef at the time, Auguste, would bring out an entree for dinner and would stand there while they tried to guess the herbs and ingredients in the food. It was such fun to watch, and Auguste would proclaim the winner, although most of the time it was a tie. There was such laughter and joy. I gave them separate bedrooms of course, but I can't help but imagine where they actually slept when the lights were turned off. After all, Jared's father was a bit of a rogue, although I never let on that I knew it."

Alice gave a small chuckle and her eyes had a merry twinkle when she said this.

"And I, well, I was once as young and beautiful as you, my dear, and there were a few wild oats sowed in me. Fortunately, the first one that took root was Jared. But as to the girl, she never came back and I never did find out what happened, but I thought that Jared was in love with her... I'm sorry, is this bothering you? I don't even know how you know Jared."

"I'm not sure yet, either," mused Dee, "Since we've only just met. He said he was bringing me here to keep me safe. I'm in some kind of trouble... I'm not even sure what it is yet, but Jared knows, and I think he's gone out on a limb to protect me." She stared off into space, wondering how close she was to the truth. Should she mention she had a husband? Maybe that was not a good idea right now.

Alice seemed to be taking her in. Her gaze traveled to Dee's fingers, resting on the expensive rings and diamond solitaire, but she didn't ask any questions about Dee's marital status or anything else of substance. Instead she asked, "Do you have any belongings? I don't remember seeing Jared drop off any luggage, now, did I?"

Dee sat there on the brightly printed sofa and looked at her solemnly. "I left the Bahamas with a small valise, but I haven't seen it since I arrived. I think Jared may have left it with your very large butler. Other than that, I have the clothes I am wearing and my handbag." She pulled out a tiny pink Chanel wallet and held it up for Alice to see. She peeked inside to check that her credit cards were there and they were. But what would happen if Steve was looking for her, and she began charging new clothes on her cards? It wouldn't take long for him to find her, would it?

An observant Alice quickly picked up on her hesitation. Without missing a beat, she said, "Let's save the shopping trip for another day, shall we? You may shop in my closet, my dear, if you haven't brought along the right articles for this time of year in Washington. I have plenty of lovely things that will fit you. We'll finish our tea and coffee, and then I will show you to your room and you can have a nice bath and a rest. Afterwards, we will decide what to do with the rest of our day."

Dee's smile was mixed with equal parts of exhaustion and appreciation—she was grateful to Jared and Alice for looking after her safety. She was in the hands of two strangers, but she felt safer than she had with Steve—safer than she'd felt in the last four years.

She decided to skip the bath and stretched out briefly on the bed to think. She was asleep in less than a minute. When she awoke she found a note on the dresser telling her that dinner was at seven. She looked around for her suitcase and found that it was empty. She tried the closet and found her wardrobe there, neatly laid out. Hmmm... It all looked so gaudy somehow. She wanted to be her old self again, elegant, intelligent, the manager of a successful art gallery. She made up her mind and headed out the door to find Alice. What she ran into was the immense presence of Samuel.

"Ah, Miss Dee," he rumbled, "Clarissa laid out your clothes in your closet, but Lady Alice has included some additions for you to consider."

"Oh," said Dee, "I didn't notice them."

"They're in the other closet," he said, smiling.

"Thank you, Samuel," was all she could muster and retreated to her room. The first door she opened was the bathroom, complete with a huge claw footed tub. "Clothes be damned," she said and stripped off her top and shorts. As she sank into an unbelievably blissful bubble bath she wondered what she had gotten herself into, and then she let herself relax in the warmth of the bath. She leaned back and thought about Jared. She almost laughed out loud when she thought how easily he had disposed of Steve's hired muscle. Then she did laugh when she remembered that she had been instrumental in dispatching the larger one. "Bastard," she thought, rubbing her arm.

So what's really going on? she wondered. *Why did Leah ask what's-his-name to call Jared? Why did Jared decide to do this? What's he going to do? What's Steve going to do? What's going to happen when they meet?*

That thought stopped her cold. *Oh shit! An immoveable object and an irresistible force.* "Who would win?" she said aloud.

Then she thought about the look in Jared's eyes when he told her he would take her away from Steve—the look that almost made her feel sorry for Steve. Her eyes softened. "Jared," she thought.

But what was it behind his eyes that she couldn't fathom? That one time when she had looked into them they said he wanted to tell her something but couldn't bring himself to do it. What was that? Something about the girl that Alice had told her about? So many unanswered questions. She sank back in the bath and tried again to relax.

"All good things must come to an end," she finally said to herself, climbing out of the tub.

"Okay, let's see what I've got here." She went to the other closet and found some stunning designer dresses. She tried on an elegant gown that fit her perfectly.

"Oh, my," she said out loud, "This one is gorgeous. I think I'll wear it to dinner."

When she checked her own luggage she found that Smaller hadn't included bra or panties when he packed her clothes on the boat. She was shocked! And then a wicked smile came over her face.

Okay, a beautiful dress with nothing under it. Let's see if Jared notices! I'm sure he will. I hope he does. What the hell am I doing? She thought finally. *Damn!* But she put the dress on anyway and headed down for dinner. Jared and Alice greeted her graciously and Dee could see Jared's eyes widen when he saw her. She watched as he took several deep breaths. *Well then,* she thought, *he did notice.*

Clarissa brought in the first course: a delicious antipasto. She was so petite that Dee couldn't believe she could possibly be Samuel's wife. Clarissa was also in the early stages of pregnancy, which intrigued Dee even more. It was a delicious antipasto. The next course was veal saltimbocca. Dee had never tasted anything this good, although she knew the recipe and had actually made it several times herself. She looked up and saw Clarissa, Alice, and Jared watching her.

"There's something here other than the normal ingredients," she ventured, summoning all of her taste buds to the fore. "Sage and perhaps oregano and a hint of anchovy?"

"Very good," said Clarissa, "Most people can't recognize those flavors under the capers." Dee noted a slight Caribbean accent in her voice. But her attention was really on Jared, who was still staring at her.

"Could you do that?" she asked, teasing him.

"Of course he can," said Clarissa, "It's his favorite dish. I make it for him every time he comes home. But it took him two tries to identify the oregano."

When dinner was over, the three sat chatting amiably as Samuel served tiny glasses of Grand Marnier and then disappeared. Words were spoken softly, but little of consequence was said. Alice was the first to retire. As she stood, Jared stood too, and kissed his mother lightly on the cheek.

"Sleep well, dear Alice, and take good care of our girl here, okay?" He tried to keep his voice light, but Dee could see and feel the undertone of worry. Jared sat down and looked long and hard at her until she wanted to escape his gaze and look away, but she couldn't. What did he want to say? She tried and failed to read something into that look. She knew so little about him... and yet so much.

Several times he started to talk, and then he would look away and then back at her. It was as if he was trying to compose himself, Dee thought quietly. She could see that this man, who was so strong that he was able to rescue her from a band of seagoing thugs, was actually suffering right at this moment. His strong hands reached out to hers, and she took them in her slender fingers and met his silent gaze.

"Dee," he finally said. "I know what I'm dealing with, but I haven't got enough information yet to decide how to handle it. All I know for sure is that what I've done so far has put you in danger and I didn't mean for that to happen. I let myself be drawn into an adventure, but now it has become very serious. So stay here, don't call anyone, don't use credit cards, and don't do anything that could help Steve find you. If he does, Samuel will protect you, but I don't want it to come to that. I won't come back until I know I can keep you safe from harm."

She started to protest and then thought better of it. Suddenly

Jared was on his feet, leaning over her. The kiss was quick and sweet. "I love you, Dee," he whispered, and then he was gone. She was alone in the lovely little sitting room: alone with her thoughts, alone and wondering what had happened to her in the last two days.

Jared dropped the briefcase off at his security firm in nearby Four Mile Run. Melanie, who ran it for him, said she'd have it open within the hour. Jared spent the time exercising in the health club annex. When he was done and showered, Melanie was ready with her response.

"Interesting case, boss. Did you know there's a kilo bar of pure gold in with the documents?"

Jared perused the documents and whistled.

"Did you read these?" he asked Melanie.

"I stopped when I saw how sensitive they were."

"I trust you, Melanie. Make a set of copies and put them in the safe. Check the originals for fingerprints and then send, no, courier them over to Stanley."

"Done," said Melanie.

And then he left for New York to see Bart.

Chapter 9

Steve, NYC

STEVE MILAN WAS ANGRY—ANGRIER THAN he'd been in a long time. He paced the length of his Soho loft, running his free hand through his hair, his voice rising higher and higher with each phone call. No one knew anything! Or no one was telling him anything. He was shouting now, shouting into his phone and yelling obscenities at the investigator who ran his private show in the Bahamas and Miami. Where the hell was Dee? More important, where the hell was the briefcase? He had his people search Nassau without results. It was as though Luddites had resurfaced and thrown wrenches into his life. What the hell was going on?

He hired a private detective who specialized in anything involving Miami and expensive boats and then waited impatiently for results. Frank Johnson did his thing; he worked meticulously, thoroughly, and came up with nada. Until, like the forty-niners in California, he panned one last stream and there was the nugget. It was in the Old Salt Bar in Miami and he just happened to ask the right question at the right time to the right person.

"Big wooden ketch? Yeah, I know her, one hell of a sailboat even if she is a deepwater boat. Name of 'Katch-oo' or somethin' like that. Goes to windward like a cat with its tail on fire. What? Yeah, she was here for a while. Then Barney Rubble came and sailed her outta here by hisself. Can you believe that name? He's a big guy, a grinder on ocean races. But he does know how to sail the big boats. No, I don't know where she went. Barney? Well, he's part of the permanent crew when she races. Tried to get into that crew meself, but didn't make the cut. Almost, but not quite."

By this time he was getting all wound up.

"If you want to sail with Herreshoff you have to be the best. When he turned me down, he give me a good recommendation, though, and now I'm sailing with a good crew and we earn our money. Not as good as his though. His name again? Herreshoff. Why do you want to know that? Everybody who sails knows him. He has to be seen to be believed. Reminds me of stories of the old whaling captains that used to hunt the whale between Greenland and Baffin Island. Fire in his eyes that makes a crewman work harder than he ever thought he could. They know it and the way they swagger shows it and we all know they earned it. I don't begrudge them anything. Herreshoff? How the hell would I know how to spell it? Figger it out for yourself!"

Frank paid the bill and twenty seconds later he was on the phone to Steve.

Chapter 10

Waiting in DC

ALONE IN THE PRETTY SITTING room, Dee thought about her love life since coming of age in her teens. First came the delight in discovering you can see into someone else's heart, and he into yours. It was a time of innocent love, based not so much on physical intimacy, but rather on a sweet give and take of affection and an unfulfilled yearning for more.

With a sigh she remembered that love did not stay like that for long. She thought about some of her experiences in high school, when the boys always wanted more than the girls were willing to give. One event, when she was about seventeen, came sharply into focus. She was at the Ranch Bar and Grill with her girlfriends, flirting with a guy she had a crush on. He'd followed her out to the parking lot and started kissing her and then groping her. He was almost out of control and she was scared, with no idea of how to stop his advances. She remembered feeling lucky that her friends arrived just in time to keep her from unraveling completely. *It could have turned out much worse,* she thought. *What was I thinking?* It was the first time that Dee had experienced lust, and it left her a more cautious person than she'd been before.

What did she want out of love? It was a question she wondered about as she dated in college and still thought about when her first marriage failed. She was an intelligent woman, so why did she have this blind spot the size of a barn when it came to love? Was it possible to have it all in a relationship or a marriage? It seemed to Dee that she was always the one who had to change, while the men she was with were allowed to stay just as they were. She found that when she tried to please a husband or boyfriend, he took advantage of her. And when she tried to stand up for herself, she was called a "ballbuster." Of course, neither way worked for her. Sometimes she just didn't know what to do.

What it came down to, Dee thought, was that perfect combination of the purity of young love, combined with a fulfilling and mature sensual love—and for some reason that had always been beyond her reach. For a moment she allowed herself the luxury of imagining a future with Jared. Then reality set in. She had no future, none at all if Steve found her. If she did anything to cross Steve, he would never forgive her, and because of that he would do his best to ruin her life, of that she was certain. He would leave her alone and ruined, and no one on this earth would be able to protect her.

But what about Jared? He was a handsome man, an amazing sailor, and the most exquisite lover, but did he have the kind of power needed to save her from Steve? She thought she could be falling in love with Jared, but she could not allow herself to imagine that he could also be her savior.

Alone and exhausted, she left the picture-perfect sunroom and made her way to the bedroom. The sheets were crisp and cool and she tried first one position and then another to get comfortable. Nothing worked. She was wide awake, and once again she found herself thinking about her childhood. It was where she always went when she was troubled. Suddenly she was three and a half again and stomping her foot on the front porch. Mother was making one of her infrequent visits to the farm and was scolding Dee for messing in the freshly picked vegetables. Dee's body language said it all: she was not going to be told anything by her mother of all people. "My grandmother loves me even when I'm bad," she said in her most defiant tone.

Dee sat bolt upright in bed. "I haven't thought of that in years!" Then she realized the significance of what she had said at such a young age. Her grandmother had always given her unconditional love—but her mother had not. Mother had always conditioned her love to something: to good behavior, to respectful behavior, and later on to good grades and success in school. Her grandmother simply loved her for who she was. It didn't take long for Dee to make the love connection. Steve loved her only when she was his dressed-up doll, smiling inanely as he tried to sound important. And Andy was even worse—he loved her only when she took care of him.

Could it be that all she really wanted was for someone to love her the same way her grandmother loved her such a long time ago? And, if that were the case, could Jared be that person? He'd just told her he loved her. But did that mean he loved her no matter what? Did it mean he would still love her even when she wasn't trying to be perfect? If she was silly or naughty or in a bad mood would he still love her? Not just put up with her, but really still love her? It was all too much to take in. As sleep started to take over, she thought the ramifications of this could be enormous. It could change her life, she thought happily, peacefully, suddenly sleepy. She curled herself around a spare pillow and closed her eyes.

She was disoriented when she awoke in the comfortable bed with its fluffy pillows and down comforter. She hadn't slept so soundly in years. Sunlight streamed in through the window, and she stretched lazily; then she dressed in soft leggings and a large shirt and pulled her hair into a ponytail, as she had as a child. She needed to exercise, to run, to laugh, to throw her arms into the air; there was too much joy inside her that she couldn't contain it. She headed out the front door. How could she know that two of Steve's men were hiding in the bushes of the house next door? In her joy at experiencing the beautiful morning, she had ignored Jared's warnings. She never saw the other two men who moved off silently, following her a short distance behind.

When she got back to the townhouse, she showered and dressed. Downstairs she found breakfast laid out on the dining sideboard, but no one was around. She wasn't even sure what day it was—Thursday, Friday? Nor could she guess the hour. Either she was too early for Alice, or too late. She poured coffee from a warming pot and selected some fruit and a warm roll filled with walnuts and raisins. She took a deep breath and slowly began to eat, and as she ate she thought about what was happening. Not always the most logical person, Dee decided that this was the time to try to put the events of the past few days into some order, and to figure out what she knew and what she didn't know.

First, Steve was probably back in New York, and was most likely very angry, wondering where she was and thinking that she was part of his problem. Therefore, he would be looking for her, and when he found her, it wasn't going to be pretty. So, she had to avoid Steve at all costs.

Second, Jared was no accident. He had been sent to look after her, but why? What kind of danger or trouble did he think she was in? Surely it must relate to Steve's export business, because Steve was always into one money-making deal or another… and most likely, they were shady deals. Shady deals meant that someone in Washington had his eye out for Steve and wanted this whole business stopped.

But where did she come in? Was she just in the way? Surely that was not part of any plan to put Steve out of business? Or, if they put him behind bars, would she be implicated because she was his wife?

All at once her mind returned to the conversation she'd had with Jared as the jet began to descend into DC. What had he said? She thought, "Exculpate the husband or extricate the sister." The SISTER… that's what it was. The idea—the request—had come from Leah! Leah either wanted her out of her marriage to Steve or was worried enough about Dee to want her out of harm's way.

Had Steve committed a crime and was he about to be arrested? Was that why they needed to get Dee out of the way? She was confused. But if that's what it was, why had Jared just told her he loved her? And was Jared now going to put himself in danger for her? If he was going to find Steve, he most certainly was putting himself in danger, because Steve never went anywhere without his thugs. She shuddered, thinking she should warn Jared.

But first she had to talk to Leah. Where was her phone? Thank goodness it was still safe in her bag, with a small amount of charge left. She hit the button to call Leah, but there was no answer on her cell phone. Without thinking, she dialed Leah's house phone. This time Leah answered.

"Dee, where *are* you? Are you okay?"

"I'm fine. I'm in DC, at a friend's house," said Dee quickly.

"I've been so worried about you," whispered Leah. "Steve's been calling here every couple of hours, day and night, saying terrible things about you. He says you stole something from him and that you're out to get him, and that when he finds you, you're going to pay! What is going on, Dee? What the hell is going on?"

"Oh my God, Leah, it's nothing like that! We were on the boat in Miami. Steve left suddenly, and then I was kidnapped by his thugs. Kidnapped, Leah! I didn't do anything wrong. He sent those awful men of his to kidnap me!" Dee stopped, sure that she was hearing clicks on the line. "Leah, Leah, are you hearing something?"

"Yes, Dee, get off the phone. Get off the phone right now! I love you, Dee. I love you, do you hear? Take care of yourself. Get away from there right now!"

Ken and Larry waited for a little while once Dee had returned to the house; then they walked confidently up to the brownstone, pressed the bell, and waited. To their surprise, the latch was released and they entered. They looked at each other apprehensively, because they had heard about what had happened to their colleagues in Nassau.

Their surprise at the size of the man who stood there froze them for an instant. It was just long enough. Samuel wasn't just big; he had amazing reflexes. Ken and Larry helped out by starting to open their sport coats, but when they reached for their guns, they were already in Samuel's hands.

"I don't think you'll be needing these," he said, amiably. "I do hope that you have permits to carry them near the capital of our country. Now state your business."

"We're here to get Dee Milan," blurted Larry.

"Get?" said Samuel. "Get!" Samuel put about half of his impressive lung power into that last statement.

This wasn't going well for Ken and Larry. "Look, we know she's here and we're trying to make this easier for everyone concerned. Steve wants her back and that's what we're here for," said Ken, smiling, knowing that it wasn't going to work and trying to find a way out of this.

Samuel didn't smile; he just stared at them. An uneasy silence developed. Finally it was broken by the arrival of two other gentlemen who identified themselves as off-duty policemen. Samuel handed the officers the guns, and then the fun began. Ken tried to run but was tripped down the stairs. Larry threw his best punch at Samuel, but he might as well have tried to hit the Washington Monument. Samuel grabbed his tie and lifted him up with one hand.

All resistance ceased.

"Show us the permits for these weapons, please," said the first officer.

Ken and Larry made no response. After all, they had just flown down from New York, had checked their bags with the guns in them like good little boys, had collected them at the baggage carousel, and thought this was going to be a piece of cake. Wrong! Handcuffs were produced and implemented. Words such as, "You have the right to remain silent... " were spoken. Ken and Larry were escorted away.

The Hammond brothers met a similar fate at Leah's apartment at roughly the same time.

Steve waited for the call that never came.

Chapter 11

Jared in New York

A T ABOUT THE SAME TIME Dee was hanging up from her hurried call to Leah, Jared, clean-shaven and looking elegant in a charcoal gray suit, was entering the offices of his Manhattan legal team. At midnight the previous evening he had called Bart Hansen's private line and asked him to clear the decks for a morning meeting. Bart had taken the request seriously, and the team was ready and able to handle anything Jared could throw at them. They'd done this before, and that's why Jared considered them to be indispensable.

Bart's secretary hurried in with coffee for everyone, and then quietly closed the door behind her. Bart took a sip, cleared his throat, and started.

"Jared wishes Dorothy Barbara to be divorced from Steve Milan as soon as possible." He passed copies of a blue folder around the table. "While this could be accomplished in Guam or the Dominican Republic, we have opted for an in-country option—namely, Las Vegas. It suits us because Steve already has a residence there, and we can 'prove' he's been in residence there since his last business trip. Incidentally, his wife has no knowledge of this particular residence." Bart aimed his pen at one of the younger lawyers on his team and gave instructions to have more papers prepared. The young man left the conference room as if he were on fire. The conversation continued in hushed tones.

Bart pulled out a second set of folders containing financial documents—mostly bank accounts and a handful of customs forms detailing current transactions. Jared sent another young lawyer out to scan those and to send them to Stanley for analysis. Then Bart dropped his bombshell.

"Did you know, Jared," he asked, "that Steve Milan recently took out a two-and-a-half-million-dollar life insurance policy on Dorothy Barbara?"

Jared almost jumped out of his chair. It all came together in a rush. Steve had planned to spend a week on his yacht with Dee. He hadn't taken a vacation in years, so why now? There would have been a fishing trip to the Bahamas, dangerously high waves, a beautiful young lady overboard, a call to the Coast Guard for help, and a crying husband mourning his lovely wife—and then a greedy Steve would collect the insurance money when things quieted down. He could leave the *Esmeralda* in Nassau. But the stupidity of one of his New York employees had him running back to the office before he could complete his plan. No wonder Steve wanted to find Dee so badly right now. Dee was in much greater danger than Jared had ever thought.

Bart watched Jared with alarm as Jared put his coffee cup down very gently into its saucer. Witnessing Jared's strength and control while he performed that simple task was frightening. Bart was even more alarmed when he looked into Jared's eyes, afraid of what he might ask him to do. What he saw there was resolve, a resolve hardening like a red-hot steel blade being quenched in oil. Bart was very glad that he was not Steve at that moment, nor anywhere near him.

At last Jared seemed to relax and spoke. "All right, Bart, see that what I have asked you to do will be done. In addition, track down any accounts Steve has set up in Dorothy Barbara's name. When you have, set up a new account in her name and prepare to transfer the monies to that account. I'll get her to sign all the necessary paperwork."

Jared rose and shook Bart's hand. "Thank you, as always, for your assistance in this matter. It is very important to me." Bart watched him leave the conference room. In all of the years he had dealt with Jared, he had never seen him so intense. Heretofore, it had always been a game—a game to make a group of entrepreneurs (and his friends) very wealthy. But this was different. Now Jared was marshaling his formidable talents to destroy. Bart almost felt sorry for Steve, but then he thought about what Steve had done and was planning to do, and he smiled.

This Steve was in for a very, very rude surprise.

Chapter 12

The Farm, Hudson, NY

Twenty-four hours earlier, Jared had left Bart's office determined to put an end to Steve. He was angrier than he'd been in a long time. But his anger was miniscule in comparison to his concern for Dee. He had to get her out of DC as quickly as possible, and take her somewhere safe from Steve and his thugs. It would also give him a chance to think and plan. He couldn't kill Steve, but he could ruin him, and that plan was rapidly forming in his brain.

Dee stood atop a little knoll, surveying the land around her, tears glistening in the corners of her eyes. Jared held her, silent, his arms encircling her waist, supporting her, giving her warmth against the cool September day. She rocked a little, then sighed, and finally spoke.

"How did you know about this place?"

"Leah," he said simply.

"Of course," came her soft reply. "It would have to be Leah. No one else remembers or cares, but Leah did. She never lived here, but she visited later on, and she knew how much this place meant to me. It was part of every childhood conversation, every childhood game we played. The farm, the farm... sometimes it was all I talked about."

Jared choked up too, and chills ran up and down his arms as he listened to her. In those few words she had touched a place in his heart that had been closed for so many years.

"Let's walk a little, shall we?" she asked. She took the little dirt road that divided the house from the outbuildings. She had likely walked the dusty dirt road as a child.

"My love of coffee comes from my grandma," she said. "I used to stand in front of the stove and say 'cook, cook, coffee.'" She cradled the store-bought latte Jared had bought her on the way from the airport.

"And your love of nature, of the simpler things in life," said Jared, with his arm around her shoulder as she walked around the overgrown property. At first he thought it was merely aimless wandering, but then he realized she was retracing her childhood steps, up paths that she remembered. She found the berry patch, then found a different path that wound around and came directly into the kitchen garden. It was all grown over now, the house having burned a long time ago, but the outlines of the various outbuildings and gardens were still visible. Dee reached down and picked up a tiny metal trowel nestled among the weeds.

"This was mine," she said softly. "It was part of a set I got for my birthday the year I turned three. I loved the tiny rows of carrots. I loved to weed them, and how I loved to pull them from the soil when I could see that they were grown." She cleaned the leaves from the toy and slipped it into her jacket pocket.

Jared said little. He knew he'd done the right thing by taking her here. It was bringing peace to both of them, at least for the moment.

Dee was talking again and Jared focused on what she was saying. "My Grandma died when I was in college," she told him. "No one knew exactly what happened. My mother called to tell me they'd taken her to the hospital, thinking she needed surgery, but she didn't make it through. They never went to doctors, and were probably afraid of hospitals, so it must have been serious. She would have been in her late seventies by that time."

"And your grandfather?" he asked.

"Eighty years old that summer; he died of a broken heart. He said he didn't want to go on without her."

More silence as she wandered, crossing the little road again to kick dirt at the site of the old barn. "I loved the cows," she said. "Rosie. Rosie was my favorite. I'd call to my grandfather, 'See, Grandpa, Rosie's looking at me with those big brown eyes of hers. She wants you to milk her now.' I must have been such a little pest, but they were so kind and patient with me. Oh, how I loved those two."

Tears formed in her eyes again and in Jared's. He suddenly realized he wanted to give this place to Dee, somehow give it back to her and preserve it for her, as if it could bring back her memories and all the love that came with it. Where she walked, Jared followed, wondering idly where the boundaries to the land were and who owned it. He made a mental note to call Bart.

She stopped suddenly, let go of his hand, and put her arms around his neck, reaching her whole body up to embrace him. Her kiss was soft at first, and then all at once it was warm and passionate. He tightened his grasp and held her face to his, responding with an urge that had been building all morning. They had not kissed like this since Miami. My God, was that only one week ago? He deepened his kiss, and she responded, her body warming to his touch, to his nearness, to his love.

Dee broke the kiss eventually, and her eyes, now unfocused, looked up at him, registering the raw emotion she saw in his face.

"Thank you, Jared," she said. "Thank you for this." She took his hand and led him gently to the rental car parked nearby. A comfortable silence filled the car as he skillfully navigated the country roads. As they went through a gate and up a long drive, she broke out of her reverie.

"Where are you taking me now?"

"You'll be safe here," he answered. "It's a bed and breakfast owned by cousins on my mother's side. Call them Aunt Em and Uncle Henry. They look like friendly old country folks, but the place has a wide lawn perfect for safe surveillance of the countryside, and Henry's country ways include the fact that he's a deputy sheriff. And so is Aunt Em." Jared knew it was probably the most he'd said all morning. The wheels of the rental car crunched to a stop in the gravel parking area, and he led her to a century-old building high on a hill overlooking the Hudson River.

———

"Jared, it's beautiful," Dee sighed.

"I know you'll be safe here," he responded. "That's the only thing that counts right now."

Later, settled on the porch with steaming cups of mulled wine, he brought her up to date.

"Dee, I'm going to be blunt about this. Your husband," he said gritting his teeth, "is a piece of work." She nodded. "His company, Electronics Experts, does some legitimate trade with foreign nationals, but that's not where the bulk of his income comes from. He's developed quite a following among 'importers' who want information they're not supposed to have. And Steve has just enough smarts, and just the right contacts, to deliver what they want. In fact, his favorite way of getting nice people to give him secrets is by sleeping with their wives and then blackmailing them until they give him what he asks for."

Her face twisted into a grimace. "Oh my God," she exhaled slowly. "Those poor people."

Jared continued. "That's how your dear husband originally came to the attention of Washington circles. It wasn't because of his foreign trade business, it was because of his illegal business in selling ITAR-prohibited information and products. You know how the gossip circles operate in Washington. He tried to pull his little scheme on the wife of a diplomat, and she was smart enough—and brave enough—to turn him down. Then she told her friends to watch out for this sleaze. One of those friends happened to be Leah."

"Oh, my God. All those business trips to Washington! I suspected he was playing around, but I never expected this."

"Believe me, I don't enjoy telling you. It's because of Leah that you came to my attention in the first place. Remember Stanley? Well, they all run in the same social circles. Leah was concerned for your safety, so she told Stanley's wife, hoping he could help, and he did. He asked me to help one night recently at dinner, and I was intrigued. But I never realized how quickly the whole episode could escalate. You see, when Steve was rejected by the lady in question, it didn't take him long to make the connection—so Leah's in danger too. I have people watching her house to protect her from his thugs. He'll send a new pair, the same way he sent them to the Bahamas and to my mother's house in DC. He has a seemingly endless supply."

She sat there trying to process it all, and then asked the one question that was on her mind.

"Where is he now, Jared? And what is he planning?"

"Oh, your Steve has been a busy boy. We've been watching him and it looks like he's on his way to Vegas. He's messed up in New York and Washington for the time being, so he's going back to a deal that's been on the back burner. It's not an easy one, because it involves winning the confidence of a wealthy and powerful man who runs the 'electronics importing' business in Morocco." At the word 'Morocco' Dee's head snapped up.

"That's what he was talking about on the phone the night he left Miami in such a hurry!"

He continued. "He has an apartment right off the strip, and he's called the super there and told him to get the place ready." She did a double take at the news of this unknown asset.

"We think he's going to make contact with a middleman. We

won't know any more until we're on the ground in Vegas. That's why I'm going to leave you here with Aunt Em and Henry the deputy sheriff. You'll be safe and I won't worry about you while I'm taking care of business."

"How long, Jared?"

"Maybe a week. I don't know for sure. You can go out and about with Aunt Em when she goes shopping. Use this card for purchases – it can't be traced. Dress comfortably, wear sunglasses and cover your hair with a scarf. Better yet, darken your hair a little if you think it suits you. Blend in with the locals and get some rest. I'll call you when I can, and send for you when I'm ready. Is that okay?"

She nodded.

"Now let's have a wonderful dinner at a little place I know down by the river. I'll leave first thing in the morning."

She smiled; Jared was staying the night.

Later, as they entered their room, she was a little tipsy. She'd barely touched the second glass of wine, but she'd eaten little and her nerves were on edge. Once the door closed Jared folded her into his arms and swayed with her, murmuring little terms of endearment in her ear. She snuggled closer and let him hold her, feeling his warmth and his strength.

"Hold me, Jared. Never let me go," she finally whispered.

"Never," he answered. "I love you, Dee. I know it's only been a week, but I do love you. Can you trust me? This is far from over, but I need to know that you trust me. I know it's too soon to ask you to love me, but, for now, just trust that I will keep you safe."

For the second time that day she broke the embrace and looked up into his eyes. Hers were already starting to lose their focus as she thought of making love to him, but his were steely and bright, as though he was intent on scouring the room looking for enemies. Finally, he held her close. She trembled ever so slightly.

"You're cold," he said. "Let me tuck you in and warm you up."

She clung to him as he carried her to the bed; with one hand he drew the coverlet aside and gently placed her in the center. She pulled him down with her and drew his body over her, kissing him with a sudden burst of passion. As their kiss deepened her body warmed to his. He rolled onto his side, taking her with him, until they were face-to-face, still kissing and now moving together in the age-old rhythm of lovemaking. In one swift move he pulled her sweater over her head and began to undo the buttons of her blouse. Soon he found the rise of her chest and took one soft pink nipple into his mouth. She gasped and moaned softly as she felt the inner strings of passion that joined her breasts to the fire in her belly. Her body was ready for him, and Dee was ready in a way that she had never been before.

Jared paused and pushed himself on one elbow to look at her, as if taking her in.

"You are so soft, so beautiful, my lovely Dee." She had no words and reached for him again and began to unbutton and unzip his shirt and pants, as if she could do it all in one smooth motion. But of course she couldn't, and the resulting tangle of clothing and blankets left them laughing and holding each other.

Soon, their passion took hold, and he swiftly finished undressing them both, lowering himself back onto the crisp sheets and pulling the covers over them against the chill. Suddenly they were skin to skin, breathing in each other's exotic scents, touching and kissing in all their secret places. She wanted him everywhere, kissing her on her lips and then on her nipples. She begged him to enter her. He did it so quickly and so deeply that she looked up at him in surprise before she was able to follow his rhythm. Her only thought was one of complete and utter abandonment to their passion and her awe at his power. She lost count of the times she lost control before she reached her final orgasm.

Jared waited for Dee and quickly followed her lead, barely able to control himself. For a few minutes neither of them moved, waiting for their breathing to slow and the pulsing to relax. She sighed and clung to him, gently separating their bodies and settling comfortably in his arms. His passion was spent for the moment, but he knew he dare not sleep, even though he whispered sweet words to her and urged her to fall asleep in his embrace.

He had to think—to plan the next few days. There would be more time for lovemaking, and loving Dee, when she was really safe. For now, her safety was just an illusion. The next morning, he left her behind with Em and Henry, knowing the simple daily life of gathering vegetables from the garden, cooking, and helping with household chores would help put her back on an even keel after the chaos of the last week.

Only the occasional jet took off from the Columbia County airport, but the next morning Jared's was one of them, and it was getting a lot of attention from the locals. Arriving in his rental car, he had been on the phone since leaving the warmth of Dee's bed. His first call was to Bart, then another to Stanley, and then a third to Melanie. He was still on the phone with Melanie as he climbed the stairs into the waiting jet. He greeted the pilots with a friendly wave, indicating he'd be with them shortly. For them, it was simply another flight to Vegas, but for Jared, he felt as though his entire life—his entire future—was riding on the success of this trip.

Steve was furious now. The briefcase was gone and so was Dee. He pulled out all the stops. He hired as many investigators as he could get to find her. "Start with that Herreshoff woman you found out about in DC," he ordered. "Track down every living relative. Find her!"

The search went on until it trickled down to a traffic cop who did part-time security work for local businesses in upstate New York, one of which was Aunt Em and Henry's. "Now that I think of it," he drawled, "There's a woman matching the description who just showed up there for a vacation a few days ago. And she's still here."

The news rocketed back up the line to Steve.

Chapter 13

Leila in Las Vegas

L EILA FELT THE JETLINER'S DESCENT and looked out into the night sky, the lights of Las Vegas visible in the distance. She remembered how excited she used to be when she was only twenty-one and Daddy let her come here by herself for the first time. It had been a long trip from Morocco, flying commercial first class because Daddy had taken the family jet to Moscow. She'd stayed in a hotel for the first week while she looked for a penthouse that Daddy said was to be her birthday present. It was the first time he'd let her out of his sight and she was both giddy and afraid. And she didn't really believe that he wasn't watching. Money had never meant anything special to her, given that she'd had all she ever needed since she was old enough to remember. What she hadn't had was freedom.

She had chosen a furnished penthouse overlooking the strip. It was all glass and modern furniture, with advanced communications technology so that she could dial up her father and chat with him whenever she wanted. Those first few trips had been for Leila's pure pleasure, since Daddy wanted her to become familiar with Vegas and the people who owned it. He let her do what she wanted, including bedding a Chippendale dancer, an aspiring young model and a Hollywood actor, all the while monitoring her every move. He arranged for her to have private dinners with hotel owners and behind-the-scenes money movers. That had been her introduction to Las Vegas. But those years of fun and training were over, and Leila, now twenty-six, was ready to become her father's junior partner.

The name of her first assignment was Steve Milan, and her father gave her a detailed briefing before she left Morocco. Daddy had called her to his palace, ordered tea and biscuits for the two of them, closed the door, and handed her a folder with all of the information he thought she would need. He told her that Steve had been nosing around him for years, wanting a bigger piece of the business in Morocco. He gave her all the technical details on Steve: bank accounts, business deals, and more. What he didn't have, he told her, was "the measure of the man." What was he like? What, especially, were his weak points? Was he trustworthy? Or was he a man of no character who would fold and leave his business partners in the lurch if things started to go wrong?

Leila was to have free rein in her character assessment, as long as she came to a conclusion that she could back up to her father's satisfaction. Whether or not they did business with Steve Milan in the future depended entirely on her judgment. And she was determined to show her father that she was ready for partnership. She knew she had only one chance.

As the flight attendants continued their series of announcements, she gathered her belongings. She'd purchased seats 1A and 1B, thinking to bring her beloved Chihuahua with her on this trip, but at the last moment she decided to leave her with her maid. The empty seat just heightened her sense of isolation. She pulled a gold-edged mirror from her purse, checking her perfect makeup. She knew she wasn't beautiful according to American standards. She was a little too dark, a little too short, and a little too thick in her hips and thighs to fit the ideal. But that did not stop the American boys from hanging around her. And they were boys, make no mistake about that, she thought.

At home in Morocco, Leila was already betrothed to a widower who was one of her father's best friends. She wondered idly if they could ever learn to love each other. She was twenty-six; he was forty-five. She respected him, as she respected her father. But love? Daddy had impressed upon her the importance of duty, and that included her promise to marry this man. Her father had gone to great lengths to make sure she was ready for marriage in every sense of the word. Leila knew how to entertain royalty, how to manage a large household staff, and how to please a man in bed. Oh, yes, Daddy had seen to every aspect of her education.

As soon as she got to her penthouse, she decided, she would read the Steve Milan brief in great detail and commit it to memory. Then she would wait for his arrival. But before he got there, she thought, she would spend a day at her favorite spa: the one at Caesar's Palace. Then she might do a little shopping.

Daddy had told her to keep a low profile. She could still be a whale, but there were to be no wild parties, no handsome young men in her bed, no heavy drinking, and, most important, no indication of her true identity. She stood in the center of her living room and hit the remote control to open the floor-to-ceiling drapes. The lights of the city filled the room with a rainbow of colors, and she let out a deep breath. *Let the games begin*, she thought. *Bring it on, Steve Milan!* All she needed now was a plan. She needed a plan to drag him in and then spit him out. She decided she would start with the premise that he was not a man of honor. Then, if he turned out to be, it would be a pleasant surprise. But the odds were against that, she mused.

Holding a soft drink on ice in one hand, she sank into one of the mammoth sofas and began to read: *Steve Milan, age forty-two, married, no children. High school education, no college. Healthy bank account, by American standards. He owned a legitimate business, but it wasn't always being used for the most legitimate purposes. Uses street thugs for enforcement. Well-groomed. Arrogant. Loved the ladies. Liked to gamble; poor loser at the high-stakes tables.*

Hmmm, this was going to be very interesting indeed.

In the end, Steve was supposed bring a tan briefcase to which only Leila knew the combination. At that point, Leila would have make the decision about whether to open it for him or not. She had seen her father place documents outlining what Steve was to do for him, contacts, and accounts from which he would get paid, along with the gold bar. Steve had already been told that if he tried to open it himself and use the information, it would immediately get back to her father and Steve would suffer a very slow and painful death. Steve had also been told that he would be contacted in Las Vegas by an unknown party to open the case. He didn't know that person was Leila.

Jared recognized Bart's ringtone on his cell phone and answered immediately. "Jared," said Bart, "we've found Steve's accounts and one of my fair-haired boys whom I can't understand most of the time has come up with a delightful way to kick him in the crotch when Steve least expects it. We don't need Dee's signature now as long as you can guarantee it before the next audit."

"Done," said Jared.

"Here's what the kid came up with: it's just beautiful! When Steve tries to withdraw above a certain amount from one of Dee's accounts, all the rest of the money from that account and all of the other accounts in her name are automatically transferred to her new account. This means whenever he checks the account up to that point, the money is there. And, if a casino puts a temporary gambling lien on his account—which they will—above the limit amount, that also triggers the transfer, including the amount under lien. Steve is screwed!!"

Jared was silent for a moment.

"I trust that you intend to reward this young genius? I would like to provide the funds."

"Naturally," said Bart.

"Suggest a figure."

Bart did so.

"Double it," said Jared.

Chapter 14

Mark, Mitch, and Melanie

MARK AND MITCH WERE EX-SEALS. *They had gone through the course at the same time and graduated with honors. Because of their mutual proficiencies, they had been assigned as security for US foreign embassies in what was considered "Countries of Extreme Risk." Commendations followed their careers. Foiled assassinations, car bomb attempts and—not the least—rescue of the daughter of the ambassador held as hostage after she had foolishly gone shopping without her guardians. For that one, Mark was awarded a purple heart, which would have been awarded posthumously if Mitch had been a fraction of a second later in putting a round into the shooter's head. They were a team. A very, very good team.*

But now they were out. They knew how good they were and Uncle Sam was not rewarding them sufficiently. And with the flush of youth, they decided to start their own security business.

So far, it had been all talk and not much business.

This Sunday found them on the beach in San Diego gearing up for a five-mile open water race just to keep fit. There were around thirty other masochists suited up for this little swim and they automatically checked each of the competitors out. Mark immediately focused on one of the females who looked like she could really go a marathon in bed. He looked her up and down with an appraising eye, and when he looked back up, they suddenly made eye contact. Oops, *thought Mark,* Screwed *again. But then she winked at him and the game was on.*

Mitch, however, had noticed one man who seemed to have gathered quite a congregation. He wondered how a guy this age would perform in the water, but decided that he was giving away ten years or more to them and wouldn't be a factor. There were a couple of others in this elite group that might give them trouble, but Mitch figured that he and Mark would use them to set the pace and finally, the race would come down to just the two of them. Again.

The race started with running into the surf and swimming out to the first deepwater buoy.

At the end of the first mile, the group was still tightly packed.

At the end of the second mile, there were nine in the lead and the rest were falling back.

At the end of the third mile, there were seven.

At the end of the fourth mile, there were four.

Mitch was pushing Mark a little because he knew that a really strong finish was not Mark's forte. But then, Mark had surprised him before. At this point in the race it was all about stamina and endurance. He really didn't care who was behind him; he was focused on the finish line ahead.

And then there was another swimmer between them. Long arms hauling a lean body through the water, strong legs driving it ahead. Mark went into overdrive and Mitch did too, but this guy was just too fast.

They lost.

But they did better their own records. And all three bettered the course record.

When the three of them staggered out of the surf, the media was there. The first comment was, "These guys pushed me past a limit I didn't know that I had." Mark and Mitch were amazed. Pictures were taken. Mark suddenly realized that there was a fourth finisher among them. And she was right next to him, holding him, it seemed, for support? He was confused. All this on just a look and a wink?

When the press was done and the picture taken for the next morning's sports section, the four of them looked at each other. "We owe you a beer," said Mitch. "I never figured you for a factor. You proved me wrong."

"That was far and away my best for this race. You paced me perfectly," the winner responded.

"About that beer," said Mark, bringing the conversation back to ground level.

"Aren't you forgetting someone?" the man asked.

Oops, again, *thought Mark.*

"Okay," said Mitch. "He's Mark and I'm Mitch, and who the hell are you?"

"My name is Jared."

"And my name is Melanie," said the woman.

And so, while Mark was enthralling Melanie with his life story, Mitch was telling Jared about their dreams of a security business. Melanie, who had been listening with half an ear to that conversation, spoke up. "First of all, you need a manager. And second, you need venture capital."

"I can make you two clowns very rich if you can find the money," she continued.

"What makes you think that?" asked Jared.

"I have an MBA from Caltech. But more than that, I'm my daddy's daughter!"

"Good enough for me; I've got the money!" said Jared.

And a business was born. That had been more than four years ago.

———

Mark and Mitch were camped out on the knoll above the bed and breakfast where Dee was staying. They, or one of their other teams, had been there around the clock for three days since Jared had called Melanie. Unlike some of his previous start-ups, Jared had not sold this one; he'd remained a minority partner. Even so, everyone knew that when he called, his word was law. As CEO, Melanie was used to getting odd calls to send her "kids," as she called them, off to strange corners of the world, or even strange corners of the US, on short notice. She now had thirty-two "Bad Boys" on her staff plus a team of computer gurus to deal with another side of the business. But Jared had been adamant. He wanted the best people for this job. Mark and Mitch and the other best teams. No one, but no one, was to get near Dee. Melanie acceded to his demands, although she was not enthusiastic about sending the father of her unborn child in harm's way.

Mitch and Mark took on the assignment with their usual professionalism. After all, when all was said and done, the business was set up and running, Melanie was making it profitable, and she was happily married to Mitch, not Mark. This one was for "The Man." If Jared wanted Dee protected, then that was what they did. They also knew that the team working around the clock to protect Leah was almost as good as they were. The second team had successfully quashed the Hammond brothers—who had been sent by Steve to harm Leah—quite easily. That's why Melanie hired them.

Mitch was scanning with his hooded binoculars. It was 01:33 by his dive watch. But Mark saw them first.

"Over there," he whispered. Mitch zeroed in. When the interior lights went on, faces were plainly visible. Mitch's binoculars had a built-in camera that was very busy at that moment. It really wasn't necessary. "Don't we know them?" said Mitch, "Pittsburgh, maybe?"

"Yeah," whispered Mark, "They really need another lesson."

"Don't forget that they are two really mean bastards and the taller one almost cut your dick off with that sleeve knife he had."

"Okay, they're out of the car and heading for Dee. I would think that if I were going to check into a B&B, I wouldn't park my car up the road and walk in at this time of night."

"We move?"

"Damn right!"

And Mitch and Mark disappeared into the night as silently as the September dew settling onto the midnight grass.

Hans and Georg split up when they got close to the house. Those really were their names since they had been born in the Pennsylvania Dutch country, which really was the Pennsylvania "Deutch" country after the original settlers' German heritage. In their misspent childhood they had abandoned the pacifist teachings of their parents and had opted for a more violent lifestyle. And they were very good at it. They didn't anticipate any problems tonight. Get in quickly, neutralize the old couple, snatch the girl and get out. Piece of cake! Hans picked the back door lock while Georg jimmied the window in the laundry room. Georg finished first because the back door didn't have a modern Schlage lock but an ancient one that needed an old-fashioned skeleton key. Hans was at his wits' end when he finally defeated it by turning the knob. It was unlocked. He quietly moved inside. And then the lights went on and he was looking at the muzzle of a double-barrel shotgun, the end of which looked to him like the tops of two black coffee cups.

"Nice of you to join us," said an elderly man. "We've been watching you come up the road. Need a room for the night?"

Dee was sleeping lightly when a fingertip touched her earlobe. At first it was annoying, just enough to wake her and then the third time she came fully awake and realized there was a man next to her on the floor.

"Get dressed!" he whispered. "Quietly!"

"Oh shit," she thought, "not again." But somehow she knew

that he was a good guy and this was serious. He was emptying her dresser into a backpack. She felt like reminding him to pack her undies and had to stop herself from laughing out loud.

Been there, done this, got the T-shirt, she thought. Strong hands eased her out the window and onto the fire escape. Down the fire escape stairs and out onto the back field she went. She was led on a circuitous route to the top of the knoll. How he had done it so soundlessly was beyond her. It was as though he put her feet down where she was weightless and no sound could be made. But then she was down on the ground on a blanket and he was looking through the scope of a sniper rifle pointed at the farmhouse. He'd made some small adjustments for windage. Dee raised an eyebrow inquisitively, so he handed her the pair of hooded binoculars. She saw Henry holding the shotgun aimed at one of the thugs and saw the other thug as well. She drew a sharp breath and was about to speak when her rescuer put his hand on her arm and shook his head. Then he leaned back to the rifle. Dee went back to viewing the scene through her binoculars.

"Drop your weapons," demanded the man, and Hans obliged. Not that he was worried; Georg was in the laundry room. "And the knife up your sleeve."

How the hell did he know about that? Thought Hans. And then Georg appeared. Hans breathed a sigh of relief, until he realized that Georg's hands were shackled behind him. Furthermore, there was a nice old lady with a vintage, genuine Colt 45 pointed at his left kidney.

The elderly man put the shotgun down and brought out his own set of handcuffs.

"Em," he said, "the sheriff deputized us seven years ago because he needed a force to protect this county in order to qualify for some sort of New York State subsidy, and no one else wanted the job. Now here we are, up to our ears in criminals and with no one to call. What, oh what, shall we do?" he asked rhetorically.

"Let's chain them to the steam pipe and go to bed and think about this, Henry," said Em. And so it was done, and Steve's two best minions spent an unpleasant night listening to the pipes knock and the giggles and moans and bed-creaks coming from the room upstairs —right above their heads. It didn't get any better the next morning when they experienced upstate New York Columbia County justice.

The man protecting Dee relaxed and started disassembling his rifle.

"Tell me that you were not the only person rescuing me and protecting Auntie Em and Henry?" whispered Dee. He said nothing but Dee felt two tiny taps on her right ankle. Dee looked back and saw the vague outline of another man.

"How the hell do you do that?"

"We practice by sneaking up on black cats at midnight. I'm Mark, by the way. And this is Mitch," said Mark. "Now let's pack up and get out of here."

He handed her the backpack with her clothes in it. Then came one of the weirdest, wildest things Dee had ever done. She was in good physical shape and running was one of her workouts, but she was not prepared for running through the woods in the dark of night. Mitch led and Mark brought up the rear. She had her hand on Mitch's back most of the time to guide her, but he seemed to be running effortlessly as though it was bright daylight. Tirelessly. Endlessly.

After what seemed like two miles (they later told her it was closer to three), they came to a dirt road where an old MGB waited. Packs went into the boot, Mitch went into the right-hand driver's side, Dee went into the passenger's seat, and Mark went into the jump seat, with his cell phone out. Her head snapped back as Mitch accelerated away. Obviously, someone had lavished loving care on this vehicle, because it was race ready. It did just that.

Finally, Mark clicked off the phone. He shouted up front to Mitch. "Albany Airport! Three tickets to Las Vegas! Melanie says to lose the hardware."

"Done," said Mitch, and at every little stream that had been grooved out by glaciers in New York during the last Ice Age, the boot was emptied.

"What happens to the car?" said Dee when they got the airport.

"Melanie will handle that," said Mitch.

"Melanie?"

"My wife, mother of my soon-to-be-born son."

Dee couldn't believe that these two incredible men would allow themselves to have some sort of real life. It didn't seem possible.

"Weapons?" asked Mitch.

"Melanie says that they are there waiting for us and we are cleared to carry. We're also okay with casino security, all along the strip."

"Works for me."

She still couldn't believe what she was hearing. She could believe the part about Steve, but that Jared could muster this kind of protection for her? How, or why, would he ever have needed it? She knew that question would have to be asked and answered before she could spend the rest of her life with him.

Chapter 15

The Flight to Vegas

DEE HAD AN AISLE SEAT in first class with Mitch in the window seat and Mark across from her. It made her feel safe even though she knew they weren't carrying any weapons. At least she thought they weren't. They seemed to be weapons unto themselves. Finally, she broke the silence, "Who are you?" she asked quietly.

Mitch answered. "Friends of Jared."

"But how does he know you? Why does he need you?"

"You mean people like us?"

"Yes."

Mitch looked at Mark and gave a slight nod. Mark took over from there and told her the story of the five-mile swim. "And so the company was born, except that Melanie fell in love with Mitch instead of me," he finished. "She was as good as her word, though, and really got the company going. In six months we had more business than we could handle, so Melanie wanted to hire some help. Mitch and I were skeptical, but she insisted.

"Where are you going to find guys as good as us?"

"Same place I got you two clowns!" she retorted.

"So she recruited Seals. But we got to 'interview' them."

"I'll bet that was fun," said Dee, impishly.

"It was, but not for them," said Mark.

"One or two of them even tapped you on the shoulder during our 'Try to sneak up on us in the middle-of-the-night' exercise," said Mitch.

"They were both good," said Mark. "That's why they're guarding Leah." Dee did a double take.

"You're guarding Leah?" she asked, no longer surprised by anything.

"Of course," said Mitch, "She got involved when she talked to Stanley's wife; then, when Steve started calling her, Jared called Melanie."

"Does she know?"

"Probably not. When we can, we prefer to remain covert. It gives us a degree of freedom if the 'prospective perpetrators' don't know we exist. If we can, we use other, more obvious assets."

"Like Samuel and those two moonlighting cops?"

"Exactly, but we were there, just in case."

If it hadn't before, the gravity of Dee's situation finally soaked into her mind. That and what had been done to protect her, without her even knowing.

"Why didn't someone tell me?" she asked.

"Jared said he tried to tell you, but things were moving too fast. I can only imagine Melanie's eyes rolling at how many miles our corporate jet has flown this week. Plus the charters. You are very, very special to us."

Dee sat back, trying to comprehend and absorb all of this. After a while she turned to Mitch and asked, "What happens in Las Vegas?"

"We're staying at the Bellagio. You need to change your looks and just disappear. However, Jared says that he wants you to be in at the end of this little gig, so we have to make you as easy to guard as possible."

"I think that you would look great as a redhead," offered Mark.

"Yuck" she said, but finally acquiesced. "All right, auburn."

"Are we trying to wave a red flag here!" said Mitch. "I'm sorry, Dee, but when we get done with you, you are going to look in the mirror and see your maiden kindergarten teacher. You are going to look terrible and we expect you to act the part."

"Oh boy," said Dee. "Now there's a role I've always wanted."

"Yes, well, it will keep you safe and you'll get to see the final act."

"Do I have to?"

"Lady, you won't believe what we all are going to have to look like and do in Vegas."

Dee sat back again. A light went on in her head. Mitch and Mark weren't treating her like she was a blonde bimbo. They were treating her as she had been treated in the art world. They had accepted her as a partner in this vignette. They respected her intelligence. Suddenly she remembered how it felt—and it was great to be back. Yes, that's what it was, she was back! There was no stopping her now. If she had to put on a disguise, so be it. That could be fun. Dangerous? Well, hell, yes, it could be. An evil smile lit up her face. She looked up at them and saw that their smiles mirrored hers.

"Welcome to the team," grinned Mitch. "Welcome to Vegas. Let's enjoy this for what it's worth." And the plane signaled its final descent into Sin City.

Bring it on, thought Dee. And she wondered at that moment where Jared was, and wondered if he was thinking about her. His boys had kept her busy on this trip, but now her mind was back on Jared, and she hoped he was safe.

"Where is he?" she asked Mitch.

"Waiting for you, of course."

The landing gear squealed as the huge jet touched down.

Chapter 16

The Bellagio

ITHOUT CHECKED LUGGAGE, THEY WHISKED through the concourse to where a stretch limo was waiting. But Mitch and Mark held Dee back and actually shielded her while a trio that looked remarkably like them boarded it. Then they ushered her to the taxi station where they took the third taxi in line. Her left eyebrow lifted.

Mitch said, "You're still too conspicuous, so we had to take precautions."

"How are the kids, Howie?" Mark asked the driver.

"Fine, and there's another one gearing up in the cockpit."

"Don't you know when to give up? Your wife should have you fixed."

"We did that to the cat and from that time on he always looked so sorrowful. I'm not having any part of fixin."

She didn't ask how many children, including the new one, Howie had fathered. "I assume he's part of the team?"

"As you noticed, one of our additional assets," said Mitch.

The taxi did not pull up to the front of the Bellagio, but rather it wound around back to the service entrance. Mitch and Mark didn't have to carry Dee in; after the nighttime run through the woods of New York, she was up to moving like a wraith. The service elevator took them to the thirty-third floor and she was hustled into a luxurious suite. She took a deep breath and looked at them.

"Okay, in sixty seconds we move to another room, right?"

"Nope, we're in for the night. Our alter egos checked in one floor down. Settle in, unpack, take a bath, come back for dinner, and then get some sleep. You have a couple of busy days coming up."

Dee noticed that there were two bedrooms in addition to the living room. "Oh, so we are now roommates?"

"Think of us as brothers."

"I never had one of those; now I'll get to find out what it's like."

"Go take a bath; you look like you could really use it."

"Thanks for your observation, mon frat. If this is what having a brother is like, I'm glad I had a sister!" she huffed and slammed the door to her bedroom. There she found the suitcase Mark had packed. It was very neatly done, and her undies were all there. "What a dear Mark was," she thought until she realized that Mark had thrown everything into a backpack, not a suitcase. And all of the clothes here were new! Someone had gone through the backpack in New York and had bought her a matching one here in Las Vegas. Who could do that? A moment's thought answered that question.

When she came back out refreshed, she was in a more forgiving mood. Then she saw the meal laid out before her. At first all she saw was the pâté de canard with toast points and a small bottle of Veuve Clicquot champagne. An exquisite flute had been poured for her. She realized she was ravenous but she managed to consume the pâté and champagne at a leisurely pace.

"You're not having any?" she asked of her newfound brothers.

"We're waiting for the main course," was the answer, "and no wine," Mark added unnecessarily.

The next course appeared magically, served by a waiter who appeared and disappeared without a sound.

"Another available asset?" she asked.

"We know who we can trust," said Mitch.

The filet of beef was wrapped in bacon and accompanied by parsley new potatoes and spring peas. The wine was Gevrey Chambertin '59, which the men looked at longingly and stoically yet declined. They ate in silence, sad that this wonderful meal was being consumed for its caloric content rather than for its gastronomic splendor. Dee looked at her glass and decided she wouldn't drink any either.

When the table was cleared, she watched the two men seeming to communicate without speech. They were obviously waiting for her to go to bed... not a bad idea, since she was exhausted. Impulsively, she gave them each a hug and went to her room.

She tried to sleep, but her mind was alive with thoughts of the events of the past week. She peeked out of her door and saw Mitch asleep on the couch. Or was he? Somehow, she didn't think so. The TV was on but the sound was off and he was just sitting there. Then she noticed he was looking right at her. His wink startled her and she quickly closed her door. He was standing watch, she realized, and she felt as though someone had hugged her. She wished it had been Jared. She shook her head and went back to bed, but sleep would not come. Her brain whirled over the events of the past few days. How long had it been? Once again she had lost track of what day it was.

She thought back to Labor Day weekend and realized that more than a week had gone by. It was Labor Day weekend when she was on the boat with Steve in Miami and he'd suddenly left for New York. Then she was with Jared, her yacht was hijacked, she was taken to the Bahamas, rescued by Jared, flown to DC to meet his mother, and ended up in New York State. And now she was in Vegas. How long? Eight or nine days? She searched in her bag for her cell phone, but the battery was dead. Not that it mattered. What did matter was that she was so far away from any life she'd ever known before. Less than two weeks ago she had been in New York, living an unsatisfying life as Steve's wife. And the worst part of that life had been Steve himself. Why had she ever married him? Her inner conversation took hold.

Looking back there were so many red flags. Why had she ignored them? Steve was not her type, but he had wooed her with promises of a wonderful life. The first red flag was that she was not at all turned on by him physically, and the so-called chemistry wasn't there. But she lied to herself and told herself that in time she would come to love him. Lie number one. It never happened. She ended up hating his touch and doing everything possible to keep his body as far away from hers as possible. She was sure this wasn't a big issue for Steve; he could find women who wanted him everywhere he went—and most likely had done exactly that. The second lie she'd told herself was that they would at least get along on an intellectual level. And of course that hadn't happened either. Steve was way too busy showing himself off, and wanted Dee at his side to look pretty, and glitzy, when he entertained customers. If she tried to say anything of merit, his first impulse was to silence her with an angry look.

Nor did she have any sort of freedom. Steve monitored her phone calls, her shopping trips—she could buy what she wanted, but who she lunched with was carefully monitored. He didn't want her to have long chats with her sister, whom he considered nosy, and he questioned her constantly about her comings and goings. The only thing she was totally free to do was to make herself beautiful and to shop. So that is what she did. Endless rounds of beauty salons, spas, fancy clothing stores, and shoe stores, so that when Steve called and told her where to meet him for dinner, she was ready. She had become a soulless, mindless Barbie doll.

Oh, God, thought Dee, *how far have I fallen? All those years of school and work to make something of myself, and this is what*

I've become? I haven't let myself think about it for four years, but look at yourself. Take a good long look at yourself, Dee! She let out a long sigh and looked around at the darkened hotel room. And now what?

She was still a married woman, and now she was far from home, and Steve most likely had his band of thugs out looking for her everywhere.

But then, without so much as a whisper or a warning, Jared had sailed into her life. By accident? Or not? But there he was—handsome, attractive, articulate and sophisticated—sweeping her off her feet. When it came to choosing her lovers, she had always been very careful. She thought back to young Dee in the parking lot, and realized how much of a turning point that had been. She had vowed never to be swept off her feet like that again, but with Jared, she had been. And she had trusted him! If she hadn't, she probably wouldn't have been able to enjoy the wonders of their first lovemaking as much as she had. It was everything rolled up into one: a powerful attraction combined with an innate trust that what they were doing was right—and yes, even good.

This is so unlike me, thought Dee, *but, if it is wrong, why does it feel so good? Why do I trust him? Could I be in love so soon? I am going on blind faith and trust,* thought Dee. *God help me if I'm wrong.*

———

After two hours of sleeplessness, Dee finally gave up and padded barefoot into the living room. The watch had changed and Mark was there. The TV was still on, but muted. She curled up on the other end of the couch from Mark. His eyes were closed.

"I knew it would be useless to try to sneak up on you," she said. "You knew I was coming. How?"

Mark's eyes opened. "Your perfume. It preceded you."

"You don't miss much."

"We try not to."

Mark closed his eyes again.

"You and Mitch like watching TV with the volume off?"

"It makes people think we're awake and it gives us enough light to 'counter the evil spirits.' It's amazing what you can hear when you are not distracted," he said.

Mark seemed relaxed, but she suddenly realized that, in relaxation, he was wound like a coiled snake ready to strike. She thought about this for a while and then quietly said, "Tell me about Jared."

He was silent for a long moment.

"Well, you know about the swim. Anyone who can whip our asses when we don't want it done, is all right in our book. But then he set us up in business. With Melanie. And she took it right over the top. She's one hell of an athlete herself, but you can't believe the regimen she put us on. Ever hear the term 'kinesthetic awareness'?"

"Yes," she said. "I did gymnastics when I was in high school. It means that you are aware of where your body is in three-dimensional space at all times."

"That's correct. It's all about balance—having your center of gravity over your center of effort at all times. Mitch and I didn't know why we were so good at what we did. Jared spelled it out for us. Must be his engineering education. Anyway, Melanie set up the training. Heaven help us, the first week was ballet school. We thought we were flexible until we met those folks; their spines are made of rubber. Then there was the gymnastics week. Melanie made a special balance beam for us. Four inches wide and thirty feet long with three hinges so that it wasn't straight. We had to walk it blindfolded! Barefoot! And there were obstacles. Little upturned tacks. A two foot section missing. My favorite was the patch of Crisco shortening about a foot long.

Did I mention that this beam was six feet off the floor? We were told it was training so we could land on our feet like cats."

Mark paused for breath and then said, "By the way, Jared shows up once a month to re-up on the training. He's been with us through all of this. He's as good as we are, if not better. If you are a bad guy, you really don't want to play games with Jared. You're safe with us, Dee, but if Jared has his arm around you, lady, you are really the safest woman on this planet!"

With that Mark gave her a look that said, "Go to bed. We're here for you; nothing is going to happen to you on our watch." And he returned his gaze to the silent TV screen.

She went back to her lonely bed and her thoughts.

Once there, she suddenly realized she wasn't alone. As a hand gently touched her shoulder, she knew it had to be Jared's.

"How?" she started to say, but even that brief word was interrupted as Mark exploded into the room. Jared blocked his first punch, and then Mark recognized him.

"Damn it, Jared, don't do that to us."

"Settle down," said Jared. "I'm supposed to be somewhere else tonight but I wanted to be here. I couldn't find a way to get a message to you in time."

"How the hell did you get in?"

"Remember the beeping horns a while ago that made you look out of the window?"

"Yes."

"Well, while your back was turned, I came into the suite."

"Shit!"

"And when Dee came out to talk to you, I got into her room."

"Shit!"

"Over and done," said Jared. "Now, Dee and I have some things to discuss and there is only so much darkness left to do it in."

Mark left, closing the door softly, but he would no doubt wake Mitch; they would both need to stay on guard.

Suddenly Jared was kissing her and she was returning his kiss, everything else forgotten. She melted into his arms and felt his body mold to hers. Quietly he lifted her off the floor and onto the huge bed without breaking the kiss. He listened for a moment and outside the dark bedroom everything was quiet. He settled her into his arms, stroking her all over, his breathing becoming rough as he became aroused. Eventually he broke the kiss and pulled away from her.

"I love you, Dee." he said.

"I love you too, Jared."

"I need to tell you what's going to happen in the next three days. And what part you have to play in it."

"No," whispered Dee, "First I want you to tell me about her."

His eyes opened wide, registering that he must have understood what she meant. She held him tightly and a very long moment passed as he stroked her gently. She could feel the pain he was suffering and her heart went out to him. She wished she hadn't asked him the question but she knew she had to. She had to know the answer, because she felt that this woman from so long ago would somehow be part of their future unless Jared could expel the old ghosts. She knew that her entire future depended on it. If he couldn't open up to her, she didn't know what she would do.

"Dee, I've never told anyone about this. No one knows the whole story. A few close friends know parts of it, but no one knows it all. It's going to be hard for me to tell, and painful for you to hear, but you need to know. You need to know what I am capable of. Once you do, if you can forgive me, then I think—no, I know—that we can be happy together, that we can have a future together. But I'm afraid of hurting you now."

She touched her fingers to his lips. She looked deep into his eyes and saw the pain written there.

"Jared, the not knowing is much worse. You need to tell me; I know that I love you, I know that I can understand."

He began to turn away, tears forming in his eyes. His voice was hoarse, but he pressed on.

"Her name was Jessica. We fell in love when I was a junior in college and she was a freshman. I was young and she was so beautiful. I was smitten from the first moment I saw her."

He continued. "She was so innocent and so trusting, and I fell for her like a ton of bricks. Up until then I'd had my little flings, but Jessica was my first true love. I couldn't eat, I couldn't sleep. All I wanted was Jessica in my arms. I knew I couldn't marry her yet, but I wanted her so badly I could think of nothing else."

Dee could see the anguish in his eyes, and she had to look away because if she saw his pain anymore she knew she would make him stop just to spare him.

"You must have known that the dress you wore at my mother's belonged to her. I saw you in it and everything came back to me that night. I brought Jessica home at Christmas because I wanted to introduce her to my parents, but also because I wanted her in my bed. I wanted to make love to her. I thought I would go mad if I didn't."

Dee turned away. He was right. This was painful for her too, but she had to hear him out.

"Oh, my mother thought she was so clever, putting us in different bedrooms, but that didn't stop us. By that time, Jessica wanted me as much as I wanted her, and we threw caution to the wind. Night after night, for almost two weeks, I came to her room and made love all night long, leaving only when it was getting light. We couldn't get enough of each other." He gave a deep sigh, as if he was letting all of the air out of his body.

"All through that winter semester we worked very hard. We saw less of each other because of it, and I could see that Jess was tired. We were so looking forward to spring break. We were going to take the train from Boston to DC to visit my parents again."

He stopped and shuddered. His whole body was trembling. Dee reached out to him, but he pulled away and began talking again, this time in a voice so low she had trouble hearing him.

"But just before we left, she asked to borrow my car so she could visit her mom. I said 'yes' even though I was uneasy with her driving my Porsche. I should have gone with her! I should have been driving that car. But I let her go alone… "

His voice cracked and Dee pulled him to her, rocking him the way she would rock a child. He pulled away and went on.

"She was hit by a drunk driver. A damned drunk driver! Can you imagine the horror? She was half an hour away from being with me, and a drunk driver in a big damned car crashed into her and crushed her! It will haunt me for the rest of my life. It haunts me that I let it happen, that I wasn't there for her, and that a drunk driver took her from me."

"Oh my God, Jared," whispered Dee. "I will never try to take her memory away. I know you loved her, and I understand. You never forget your first love, and I will never try to take her place or erase her memory."

Thinking she'd helped him, she attempted a tiny, encouraging smile, and saw in return the continued anguish in his expression.

My God, she thought, *there's more.* She kept silent and let Jared begin again.

"She wasn't merely tired that semester, Dee. She was three and a half months pregnant with the baby we'd conceived over the Christmas holidays. They found that out at the autopsy. And she never had a chance to tell me."

"Oh, Jared, I'm so sorry! I'm so very sorry! I can't imagine your pain. I can't imagine how you dealt with the pain."

This time his silence lasted a very long time. Dee was patient and held his two hands in hers, but he was not meeting her stare. He was looking down, looking away, as if the worst was yet to come.

"I ruined him. It took me four years after I graduated, but I ruined him. When I went to work for Atlantic Autopilot, I didn't realize what I was capable of doing. I rose in the company because I was always solving their business problems along with the technical ones. But my hatred for that man never diminished. When I finally knew that I could do it, I ruined him. I destroyed his company, his family, and everything that was dear to him. When I was done, I realized there were other people I had hurt in my lust for revenge. All of his employees and their families. In the moment I saw his business collapse, I saw what I had become and realized I had to control that power within me. That is what I live with every day of my life. And that is what you have to know about me if you want to share my life."

He finally looked up. Tears streamed down Dee's face. Silence engulfed them.

Finally, after what seemed like an eternity, she spoke. "Jared, my love, my darling. I can't believe the pain you've been through. I can't imagine, because I've never been through anything so terrible in my life." She stopped, knowing that she had only one chance to say it right. She began again, slowly.

"I've only known you for a little while, but I see only the good in you. I see how kind you are to everyone, to your mother and to everyone who works for you. And they love and respect you."

"And I want to spend the rest of my life with you, Dee. I love you. Now that you know everything, do you still love me?"

"Oh, yes, Jared, I do love you. Whatever happens in the future, we'll face it together. You won't be alone ever again."

His eyes hardened, "Dee, now I have to use that same power to destroy your husband. Steve has a huge life insurance policy out on you, and I need to make sure there's no way in hell he ever cashes in on it."

Her eyes opened wide. She knew that Steve was after her, but Jared had just upped the ante a thousand-fold. This was no game; this was life or death—and the life at stake was hers! Jared held her close as if to protect her.

He let out a huge sigh. She studied his face. He looked tired, but his expression showed his determination. He pulled her close to him and she snuggled in his arms. He wrapped his arms around her, kissing the top of her head.

It suddenly dawned on her that she had distracted him with her questioning, but she had no regrets. *Maybe instead of distracting him I have helped him clear his head,* she thought hopefully.

"I have no way of knowing what lies ahead, my darling, but I am glad we cleared the air about the past," she said softly to no one. He was already asleep in her arms.

Later, she awoke to a discreet knock at her door. Answering it, she discovered Mitch and Mark were there. "It's getting light; Jared should leave," Mitch said.

She looked around. Jared wasn't there. "He's gone."

Mitch turned to Mark—they just looked at each other.

Chapter 17

Everyone's in Vegas

THE SUPER HAD HEARD IT all before, but Mr. Milan was in a particularly bad mood this trip.

"Yes, Mr. Milan," he droned on, "We'll get the AC fixed. I don't know what the smell is in your sink, but I'll send the plumber right up to look at that too. I know you said you were coming, but there are only three of us to take care of the whole building."

Steve slammed down the house phone and picked up his cell. The incoming call was from his casino host at the Bellagio. Once again Steve began barking orders, not noticing the cool response he was getting from his host.

He looked around his apartment and decided it was a dump. *I should've sprung for a classier place.* And with that he headed out the door, swearing under his breath.

Running around in the back of his mind, like a rabid mouse, was the thought that he didn't have the briefcase.

Leila was getting the full treatment: manicure, pedicure, facial, massage, and removal of anything she considered excessive. The beauticians all knew her and vied to be the ones to provide her with services, given her reputation as a generous tipper. When she was ready to leave, the staff called her driver to take her home for a much-needed rest. She slept until 10 p.m., then donned one of her favorite Paris evening gowns, called her driver, and headed for the high-stakes tables at the Bellagio.

She entered the casino, knowing full well that Steve—her target—would be there. She was ready to work her magic on him. She'd use just the right combination of mysterious aloofness and sensuous charm to get him on a hook tonight, and then reel him in tomorrow night. That was the plan and she couldn't wait to be done with him.

Steve found an empty chair at a poker table and sat down, barely glancing at the other Bellagio players. He signaled the dealer that he wanted in and settled down to play. When he reached into his jacket pocket for a smoke, and was told "no," his temper flared. His luck ran cold almost immediately, and as it did, his irritation soared. He stood up, gathered his remaining chips, and sullenly went in search of a luckier table.

This trip to Vegas was not as much fun as usual, thought Steve. He wandered around, checking out the tables and watching the people, unable to make up his mind what to do next. He settled for a seat at the bar—one with a view, so he could check out the ladies. Maybe that's what he needed tonight—not a win at the tables, but a win in the sack. Yes, this view was an improvement, since now he was enjoying a sea of young beauties. He snapped his fingers for the bartender and ordered a double Scotch on the rocks. As he lifted his drink, he could swear a woman was giving him the look.

"Hot stuff," said Steve. "Come on, hot stuff! Come to Papa." He said it under his breath, hoping that the looker would notice his appreciation. She ignored him and started to chat with the bartender on her side of the bar. Steve kept on drinking, occasionally looking her way. She was hot, for sure. Not tall and leggy like the blondes he usually went for, but dark and exotic looking. He wondered idly if she had an accent. He wanted to find out. He kept thinking about bedding her, which was becoming a distraction.

He picked up his drink and changed seats when someone left the bar. Then he did it again. By the third try he was sitting next to her. She was still talking to the person on the other side of her, and was turned in that direction. This didn't worry Steve. His next move was easy. He signaled the bartender.

"A double for the beautiful lady," he told the bartender.

"No thanks," she said, finally turning in his direction. "I'm leaving."

"Oh, pretty baby," said Steve. "Where are you going? I was hoping we could get acquainted." He gave her an exaggerated wink.

"I'm going to play roulette," she said and turned briskly on her stilettos. Steve followed in her wake, breathing in the scent of her perfume and watching the sway of her hips. She never once turned to look at him. She wound her way through the crowded room until she reached her table, and he watched as the crowds seemed to part for her. *She's a looker*, he thought. He wanted her to look at him, but she was focused on the roulette wheel. From his vantage point, he tried to see what chips she was playing. Were they hundreds? No, he decided, they looked like thousand-dollar chips. *I sure know how to pick 'em*, he thought. *Rich bitch.* He watched her hips sway as she leaned over the table, and decided she'd be one hot number in his bed. But, as the hours came and went, and she kept on playing and winning, his hopes began to dwindle. Eventually he pushed his way to the back of the crowd and headed out of the hotel—and back to his apartment—alone with his worries about what he would say when he was contacted about the briefcase.

Chapter 18

The Costume Party

THE SIGN ON THE DOOR said simply "Images, Inc." Dee looked up at the sign, noted the plain off-white, windowless building right off the strip, and wondered what was going to happen next. As soon as she'd showered and had her breakfast, Mitch and Mark had hustled her downstairs in the service elevator and into a waiting black SUV. Less than ten minutes later she found herself in a group of people who were being welcomed by a waif-like young man wearing tight pants.

"Welcome, darlings," he said. "Ladies to the left, gents to the right," he continued in an almost feminine voice. "And you, my beauty... so sad that we have to make you ugly! And you two, with the baggy pants and sweats, what am I ever to do with you?" The latter was directed at two young women Dee had never seen before; they looked as baffled as she was.

Mark responded from the other side of the room. "I told you, Sammy. Make the pretty one into a mess and the two messes into pretties. Keep it simple, and get it right the first time. We don't have time for a redo. They all have to be ready to hit the casino by this evening." He disappeared into the door marked "gents."

Dee found herself, along with the two other young women, in a large, well-lit room with high ceilings and racks and racks of clothes. Along the side were chairs and lighted mirrors, making the whole place look like a staging area for fashion shows.

"Welcome, welcome, my beauties. And I use the term loosely, except for you, my dear," he said, looking at Dee. "My name is

112

Sammy. Welcome to Images, Inc., where we make you over in any image you desire. Or in your case, in the images my client desires. Bella, please bring coffee and tell the estheticians that we are ready to begin. Ladies, get yourselves over here and out of your clothes. Bras and panties only. I need to see what you look like so I can dress you for the occasion." He snapped his fingers and ended with a flourish of his arms that would have left everyone laughing if it were not for the serious matter at hand.

Dee and her new companions looked around and introduced themselves as they undressed. Blue sweats offered her hand to Dee. "Hi, my name's Karen and that's Ellen. We're 'computer techies.'"

"Dee Milan. And who do you work for?"

"Oh, you're *that* Dee. OK, that makes things much clearer. Melanie told us about you and she said this was an important, rush, and in-house job."

"I've got to meet this Melanie," said Dee.

"One hell of a woman. She recruited us right out of college, along with Irving and Edgar. Top salaries, best computers and software, the works. We even have our own office."

"So, why are you here?" asked Dee.

Karen spoke first. "I'm not so sure about me, but I know that Ellen is here because she's got a genius IQ in math and computers, and so does Irving. Me? I'm just a glorified admin type. You know, I like to organize things."

Ellen just laughed. "Melanie said she needed two women who could support what Jared needed, and we were the best she could come up with on short notice. She gave us first-class tickets, a bundle of money, and told us to go out and see what it was like to do field work. So far, it's been a real eye-opener."

From across the room came the strident voice of Sammy. "Ladies, front and center!"

Stripped of their street clothes, they stood there while Sammy inspected Karen and Ellen in their sports bras and high-rise panties. "Ladies, why are you hiding those sexy bodies under baggy jeans and sweatshirts? An outrage! We have to find fabulous evening dresses for you, and then get your hair and makeup started. And you all have to match the roles you will play tonight. You will be coached on that."

Dee, Karen, and Ellen looked at each other. Dee wasn't sure what her role was, and the other women looked just as clueless.

"You," he suddenly barked at Ellen. "Off with the bra!"

She did as he demanded, but held her hands over her breasts.

"Okay!" he said, "I've seen enough! Those 36Ds will work." He turned and barked orders to the wardrobe people. "The long white halter dress with the slit up the side and no panties. And five-inch heels."

A scribe appeared miraculously and furiously scribbled down instructions.

"Who do you want to be paired with tonight?" asked Sammy.

Ellen didn't hesitate; there was no doubt in her mind. Although they had never dated or expressed any affection for each other at work, there was only one man in this crazy field op that she wanted near her – her secret crush. "Irving," she blurted out.

"Fetch him."

And shortly, Irving appeared clad only in his boxer shorts. He was four inches shorter than Ellen in bare feet, prematurely balding, and overweight. His expression upon seeing Ellen in nothing but panties with her hands not quite covering her breasts was a sight to behold.

Dee could see the mutual attraction. First he gaped, then he covered his eyes—no doubt out of modesty for her—then he uncovered them and stared at her, his mouth open. Ellen watched all of this happen and slowly dropped her hands to her waist.

Sammy clapped his hands. "Enough. You two are perfect.

Put him in a two-piece striped suit with suspenders and wing tips. She's his bimbo and she's playing with his money. Either of you have a problem with those roles?"

Irving finally managed to close his mouth. "No," he stammered.

"None at all," she said, looking at him. Then she pointedly looked down to where another problem was rising for Irving. "None at all," she repeated.

"Okay! Out of here," said Sammy. "We have to make her a blonde and do her face and put some rouge on those nipples. They're too pale! Don't worry," he added to Irving, "You'll get plenty of chances to look down her cleavage when she's bending over placing those bets."

Then he turned his attention to Karen, who was looking a bit chagrined. "Where's the other guy?"

Edgar appeared and Sammy looked at him aghast from bottom to top when he saw the sight: giant sneakers, basketball shorts that hung low in back to reveal his callipygian cleft—otherwise known as his plumber's crack—a light sweatshirt advertising an obscure minor league baseball team, a week's stubble on his chin, scraggly mustache, and hair that had not seen a barber or shampoo for many weeks.

Sammy didn't hesitate. "Shave him, bathe him, and fumigate him!" he shouted, with more appropriate gestures. "Then burn his clothes and fix his hair and face. Make him into a rich, young executive in a three-piece suit. For her, a little black dress, heels to bring her head up to his shoulder, good jewelry, a thong for her tush, and a push-up bra for her beuuutiful boobies, please. Oh, and they're just married. Any problems with that?"

Edgar and Karen looked at each other. Whatever they had to sacrifice for the company, they would do it.

"Not a problem," they said in unison.

The first two couples now dispatched, Sammy finally turned

to Dee. "Cherie, it breaks my heart what I have to do to you. My heart is breaking." With that said, two women took Dee away to a special fitting room where she would get a fat suit to pad her hips and bust line and fat pads to be applied to her neck and cheeks.

The afternoon flew by as experts worked on the trio, turning Ellen and Karen into beauties and the beautiful Dee into an expensively dressed but frumpy, middle-aged tourist.

All three ladies, now transformed, were led into a conference room. There were snacks and drinks available, but they ate and drank little for fear of removing their carefully applied makeup. The atmosphere in the room was one of excitement and anticipation, and very little was said – until the men trooped in, looking like the proverbial deer in the headlights.

Dee saw a new Edgar from the one she had just met two hours before. He had submitted to the bathing, shaving and haircut, mostly because the lady who did it was young and wearing a low-cut top that displayed her ample bosom. He attempted to reach out to feel if they were real or synthetically enhanced, but she playfully batted his hand away.

Edgar's transformation was remarkable. Gone was the sloppy, smelly, unhygienic geek. Even his posture had changed. He now stood before them, a young executive and a happily married man. And the lovely woman now standing in front of him was Karen, who had not only disguised herself in sweats at work, but had expressed a strong dislike of Edgar. He put his arm around her and she playfully snuggled into his shoulder.

Mark was next. Two-piece suit, cut large to accommodate a pistol, which was also provided. The expensive shoes, Rolex watch, greased-back hair, and sunglasses set him off as the bodyguard. He emanated vigilance, strength, and danger. He didn't have to act any part of those.

And then came Mitch. Dee couldn't believe her eyes. He

looked like a sixty-year-old beef purveyor from Nebraska, obviously rich, with a bodyguard. His hair was gray, his posture slouched, his face wrinkled; he was clad in a three-piece suit with pocket watch and fob. His general look was one of a man in his declining years, enjoying the rest of his life with the woman he loved – namely the transformed Dee. There was no visible indication of the man who lurked beneath that disguise or of what he was capable of doing if anyone threatened her.

Irving had the worst of it—when the makeup artists were done with him, he had aged thirty years. He looked like the poster boy for incipient coronaries.

Dee watched and smiled as Irving and Ellen recognized each other. "Oh, Irving, what have they done to you?" was the first thing Ellen said.

"It will wash off," mumbled Irving, his voice faint because her hug had forced his face between her braless breasts. And because her décolletage went all the way down to her navel, he was really skin to skin with her. He gulped for air and managed to pull away far enough to look into her face.

Dee knew what he was going to say to Ellen before he said it. It was written all over their faces.

Irving heard himself say, "I love you, Ellen."

She pulled him back to her and whispered, "I love you too, Irving."

Sammy broke them apart with an admonition about ruining Irving's makeup before Irving could faint from lack of oxygen. But this didn't prevent them from kissing. Since Ellen's lips were fully six inches above Irving's, she had to bend down, which caused other things to present themselves. Irving soon had his hands full, but he rose, once again, to the occasion. After all, he had played principal trumpet in his high school band and had been called "Hot Lips" by several young ladies. Now he surprised Ellen by giving her a "Flourish and Voluntary" with his lips that made her eyes cross.

"Enough!" roared Sammy. "Makeup! Emergency repair! You two cool it for now, okay?"

It was lost on the two of them. Irving finally came to his senses and let go of her breasts.

"Damn it!" shrieked Sammy.

Dee watched all this, laughed and then gave Mitch an affectionate hug. "This is going to be fun, isn't it?"

Mitch took her arm and said in a querulous voice. "You are going to become a very wealthy woman tonight, my dear."

Then the lights dimmed and a wide-screen TV came on. It was a video, and Jared's face filled the screen. They watched as Jared told them in elaborate detail what would be expected of them tonight.

Chapter 19

Round and Round We Go

J ARED FELT LIKE THE ATHLETE before the big game or the conductor waiting to begin his symphony. All his senses were honed, his mind and body ready. In a word, his adrenaline was pumping, and he was in overdrive. Everything had been planned down to the last detail, so it was just a matter of carrying out the plan, and in a few hours Steve would leave the casino a poor man. Jared never once stopped to think whether the punishment fit the crime. Tonight, the end justified the means, and that was all he needed to remember.

The view from the Bellagio's control room was amazing, and all of the monitoring equipment had been tested and was working perfectly. One high-stakes roulette table stood empty in the center of Jared's vision, presumably waiting to be staffed by incoming croupiers. This was the table Jared had purchased from Jack Lord, the hotel's owner. Jack's Chief of Security, Trent Waters, was seated next to him. Both had their attention focused on the entrances, waiting for their key people to appear.

Trent elbowed Jared, pointing toward the main entrance; Steve was walking in, sweeping the room with his eyes. He made his way around the tables and found a seat at the bar, turning his body presumably so he could see what was going on at the other tables. He snapped his fingers to get the bartender's attention; a few seconds later a double Scotch appeared at his elbow. Steve threw a bill on the bar and focused his attention on the room. He was obviously looking for Leila.

Steve decided the mysterious woman from the night before was going to be his lucky charm and tonight would be his lucky night. She was going to be there when he won big... and then he would bed her. He would take her to his place—no, he'd get a room here—and she'd rip off that sexy black dress and would want him as much as he wanted her. "Oh, what a night, baby!" said Steve under his breath.

As if on cue, she sauntered in, looking even more unbelievably gorgeous than she had the night before. She made her way to the bar, walking right past Steve and almost touching his arm, but never looking at him. He was not about to be humbled like this, so he picked up his drink and ambled to the other side of the bar, where she was just being served her Cosmopolitan.

"Pink drink for a pretty lady," said Steve. "You're gonna be my lucky charm tonight, honey, I can feel it in my bones."

She turned her head as if seeing Steve for the very first time. "Oh, it's you... from last night. You think I make you lucky?" There was a slight accent that Steve didn't recognize, but he thought it made her even sexier.

"Yes," he said, trying to make his voice alluring. "I play, you bring me luck. You're my lucky charm, sweetheart."

Her voice softened a little and she asked him, "So what's your game tonight?"

"The big wheel—roulette!" said Steve. "I'm gonna play that baby tonight and win big. Then I gotta get back to work," he said, almost under his breath.

He started to look around and as he did, he spotted the empty table in the middle of the room. He took her hand and led her away from the bar so he could get a better look at the setup. There it was, big as life, with a sign saying, "Reserved—high-stakes table." That's what he wanted. He found a pit boss and asked what was up.

"Sir, there's a party coming in, and he asked for a table."

"Well," said Steve, "I want in."

"Okay, sir. I'll see what I can do."

Jared watched from above, pleased with the way things were going. Steve was patting Leila on the backside, and Jared could see her flinch as she looked away, then turned and smiled at Steve. And Steve had taken the bait, and wanted in on the high-stakes table. So far, so good.

The trio came in next: Mitch, dressed as the owner of a Kansas City stockyard, accompanied by his wife and his bodyguard. Steve grumbled when he saw the bodyguard, and then understood that this group was probably the reason the table was reserved. *His eyes passed right over Dee without a flicker of recognition.* The pit boss whispered something to Mitch, Mitch looked at Steve, and then the pit boss signaled to Steve to join the table play. Steve looked at Mitch suspiciously and then looked away. Mitch ignored him.

Another signal from the pit boss and a lady dealer appeared. She looked to be in her late fifties; she had that "it's been a hard life" kind of look. Jared listened in to the conversation, as the dealer, Patsy, was wired for sound, as was everyone else working for him tonight.

"Name's Patsy, folks. Welcome to the Bellagio. Table stakes are a thousand dollars, folks. Everyone okay with that? If so, let's roll." The four players took their places around the table. "Place your bets, folks," said Patsy in a husky voice, and the four of them hunkered down to play. She passed her hand over the table and said "no more bets." Round and round went the wheel and it stopped on number thirty-six. No one was even close, so Patsy hauled in the house's chips and told them it was time to place their bets.

Suddenly there was a commotion at the nearest entrance, and everyone turned to look. It was Ellen. She was hamming it up and she had a mike on as well. "No, honey, not blackjack," she said to Irving. "I hate blackjack. I want some *action*, tonight, honey. I want real action!"

As if on cue, Ellen looked up and spotted Steve and the small group around the table, and she dragged Irving along behind her. "Evening, guys," she said in her loudest voice. "We want *in*." Jared watched, slightly amused, as Steve's eyes bugged out at the sight of the buxom blonde almost falling out of her sexy white halter dress.

Patsy looked her up and down, and offered her the pink chips. "Honey, it's a grand to play, if you're up to it."

"Oh, we are up to it," said Ellen in a throaty voice, "We're *in*!" Irving handed Patsy a piece of paper, gave Ellen's boobs a loving upward glance, and told Ellen to place her first bet on number eighteen. The others followed, clustering their bets around the lady who wanted action.

"No more bets," said Patsy, and with a wave of her hand over the table, she spun the roulette wheel. Patsy was one of the best quadrant shooters in the business, and tonight she was in rare form. She was in on the ruse and had been alerted that the only ones who weren't in were Steve and Leila. All of this, of course, she kept to herself. After all, Jared would include her in the payoff when the evening was over.

Irving, however, was honing the odds by calculating the probabilities in his head and feeding the bets into Ellen's ear when she bent over to kiss him. At the beginning he needed to make sure that Ellen was winning big, since Steve was following her every move, apparently abandoning his "lucky lady" almost immediately. Steve watched his own pile of chips grow, with no idea of what he would soon be in for.

By this time the little group at the high-stakes table had begun to attract some attention, but only watchers, since the stakes were far too rich for the average Joes in the casino. Just then another twosome pushed their way to the front, and an elegant couple passed their credentials over to Patsy. Edgar and Karen had arrived. Now there were eight players plus the bodyguard, and Patsy signaled that the table was closed to further bettors.

From his position in the control room, and with his earphones on, Jared watched the game with intense interest. His eyes were on Dee, of course, although he knew that Steve would neither look at her nor recognize her. Dee played her part perfectly and remained quiet as her own unfaithful, rich, criminal of a husband placed his bets. To the crowd of watchers, it was an exciting game. Cheers went up every time a number came up and Patsy made her payoffs, and there was laughter and high-fiving all around. From their piles of chips it was evident that the beef purveyor was now losing his shirt, and so was the guy in the suit with the pretty little wife. The big winners so far was "looking-for-action" Ellen, and Steve, who was hanging onto her coattails, play by play. It seemed that she could do no wrong, and her numbers kept coming up time after time.

Steve was starting to sweat. He was up as much as half a mil. "Un-fucking-believable," he said. "Jeez, what a night!" He looked over at Leila, who was feigning interest.

What Steve didn't know was that the tide was about to turn against him, and when it did it happened so gradually that he hardly noticed when it began. Ellen began to miss a few bets, and quietly started to lose a spin here and there. But since Steve was still following her lead, he began to lose a little, too, but not much at first.

Still calling the shots from above, Jared notified the pit boss and told him to raise the table stakes. Of course, he wasn't really a pit boss but was rather a high-level casino security agent who had been specifically assigned to watch over Jared's table.

"Okay, folks," said the pit boss, "stakes are going to two grand. Everyone still in?" They nodded and placed their bets.

Steve doubled his and placed his chips right next to Ellen's. And he lost. His chips were dragged away like so much flotsam and jetsam on the outgoing tide. He'd just lost thirty or forty grand. Jared grinned, knowing there was much more to come.

Ellen kept her eye on Steve. Jared knew she was walking a fine line; he'd instructed her to mirror Steve's plays, but at the same time, it was imperative that Steve lose and lose big. It was almost time to make it happen.

Jared whispered his instructions to her through the microscopic earphone hidden in one of her earrings. "Take him down!"

Ellen silently gave the others the signal, and they placed more complicated bets, making all kinds of crazy side bets, confusing Steve, and causing him to lose track. Karen continued to win. Edgar, however, had succumbed to the free bar Scotch and lost seriously, which was fine because everyone else at the table was responsible for keeping the momentum and the enthusiasm up so that Steve wouldn't quit. Steve loosened his collar, signaled for another Scotch, patted a bored Leila on the butt once more, and placed another big, losing bet.

Just as he'd won in the beginning, he was now starting to lose, and his pile of chips went inexplicably down. There were more spins, more cheers, more high-fiving, and more drinks. Steve was drenched in sweat and starting to shake as his large pile of chips dwindled away to nothing.

In the control room, Jared finally cracked a smile after watching almost three hours of nonstop action. The end was in sight!

Chapter 20

All Over but the Shouting

STEVE WAS DOWN TO HIS last twenty thousand dollars. With two thousand-dollar spins, the end was about five minutes away if he didn't take action now. He signaled the fake pit boss and demanded another two-hundred-and-fifty-thousand-dollar marker.

"I'm sorry, sir, but you'll have to come with me to verify some things. It will only take a few minutes."

"What? Are you crazy? I'm good for this!"

"Please don't make a scene," said the pit boss in an undertone, calling for a security backup. "We're trying to make this as easy as possible, but if you insist, these gentlemen will have to accompany you."

Steve was accustomed to being on the other side of this type of discussion and couldn't believe it was happening to him. Then he looked at the men and recognized exactly who and what they were. He'd employed enough of them himself in the past, although he had to admit these guys were a lot classier than the ones he was used to dealing with. He rose, exchanged some forced pleasantries with his tablemates and left.

The tablemates shrugged and smiled at each other and resumed their game until he was out of sight. Then they let out a collective cheer and hugged each other for dear life. Leila looked around the table and gave everyone a smile, not understanding a thing, but thinking that perhaps they were happy to see Steve go. She waved good-bye, took off her sandals, and headed for the door—without a clue as to what had really just happened. But her father had trusted her to use her discretion and she decided that Steve was never going to see the inside of that briefcase.

Steve was led to a conference room and seated at one end of the table. The room was not particularly large or ornate, but rather functional and well used. Steve wondered what it was used for and then it began to dawn on him that it was meant for settling just the same sort of situations that he suspected he was now in. At the other end of the table was an unsmiling, serious, impeccably dressed man who regarded Steve with the inquisitive look of an entomologist upon discovering a new beetle before he pinned it to a board and added it to his collection.

"What's going on?" blurted Steve finally.

The entomologist regarded him for a moment longer. Then he said, "It appears, Mr. Milan, that you no longer have the funds to cover your losses. We placed a lien for the amount you borrowed, but as soon as we did it all of the monies in the account disappeared. We have seen this type of sleight of hand before and, as you can certainly understand, we are very vigilant. Now, if you can prove that you have the funds to cover your losses and can produce them forthwith, this will all be an unpleasant misunderstanding. However, with that done and your hotel bill settled, we must ask you not to visit us again."

Steve was aghast. He grabbed for his cell phone. Unfortunately, he had forgotten to charge it, something he habitually did. The entomologist gestured to one of the silent men standing in the room who produced a phone charger and plugged it in for Steve.

"We will leave you to address your financial status." And Steve was alone in the room.

From the control room, Dee and Jared now watched as Steve attacked his phone.

Jared had been involved in a start-up security company responsible for developing software that detected "pushing bets" at roulette, which had been very successful. Trent, the head of the casino's security had been involved, and with the consent of the casino, he'd participated in the beta testing. As a result, although well rewarded by his job, he had wisely bought into the start-up and was now a very wealthy man. The casino treasured him because he was literally above purchase—a rare state for the head of security in a business whose daily monetary transactions were in the millions. So when Jared asked him for a small favor, Trent was glad to oblige.

"He's going to break things," said Trent from experience. Dee and Jared were silent.

There were seven accounts in Dee's name where Steve had hidden money. Dee had mindlessly signed when they were opened, thinking they were there so she could shop. Actually, though there were some convolutions that included her shopping, money was being laundered. Steve went through all seven accounts twice. Old Mother Hubbard had more in her cupboard, relatively, than Steve did now. All of the accounts were down to their minimum balances of ten thousand dollars or less.

He exploded. He threw the phone against the wall. It bounced off and, being a well-designed product, it continued to function. The coffee service was not so lucky or robust. Jared looked at Trent with a raised eyebrow. "We'll add it to his bill," Trent said.

Steve broke more things until fatigue slowed him. Then he sat with his head in his hands, trying to figure out how this had been done to him. Then some of his anger resurfaced and he tried to determine who would do this to him. He went back and forth between these two thoughts until he was as mentally fatigued as he was physically.

"I almost feel sorry for him," said Trent, "But not quite."

"I've never seen anything like that," said Dee.

"I didn't want you to see it in the first place," said Jared. "And I really don't want you to see what happens next."

"I have to."

Jared gave her a quick hug and left the room.

The door to the room opened quietly. Steve didn't realize he was not alone until Jared sat down at the other end of the table, a manila folder in his hand, which he placed in front of him. Steve thought he was another casino employee, until he looked up and into his eyes.

"You!" he said. "Herreshoff!"

Jared nodded and the full realization struck Steve. This guy had played him like a marlin on the hook, and when he was ready, had gaffed and hauled him on board. Steve! The master manipulator! He did this to other people. No one did it to him! Until now. *Oh shit, until now...*

Steve finally focused on Jared and took a deep breath. "What do you want?"

Jared opened the folder and removed a check, which he pushed across to Steve without a word. Steve noted that it covered his losses and his hotel bill with enough left over to get him back to New York. Although he didn't want to think about what might be awaiting him there.

"What do you want?" repeated Steve.

Jared opened the folder and pushed a stack of papers toward him, again wordlessly. Steve scanned the cover page and then broke into insane laughter when he realized they were filings for his own divorce.

When he stopped, he looked at Jared, "You're going to buy her from me for this?" he said, reaching for the check. But Jared's hand was there first. "You can have the bitch! Saves me the trouble of wiring her to an anchor and dropping her overboard, although the insurance money would have been nice. She's been nothing but a pain in the ass since I married her."

Steve continued to wind up on this thesis of hatred and invective toward Dee until he looked at Jared. "You want her, you can have her!" By this time he was shrieking.

Jared hadn't said a word since he walked into the room. A vein throbbed in his forehead, but that was the only indication of what was going on in his mind.

Steve continued to look at Jared, thinking of what he would like to do to him, even flexing his muscles. Steve worked out regularly and was fit in a store-bought way. But then he saw what Jared really was: a man with a hard body; he didn't look like the guys in the gym, but he recognized it nonetheless. He didn't know that it was tempered from hours behind the wheel in a force-5 gale with only a full-reefed mizzen and a wisp of a jib up. He also saw a man of obvious intelligence, given that this man had the upper hand in this room and was probably behind his losing streak. The spirit behind those eyes bored into Steve. He was suddenly very afraid. He took one more look into Jared's eyes and then he signed the divorce papers as fast as he could write his name. Jared gathered them up and released the check. And then he left the room as silently as he had arrived.

Steve felt like pinching himself to see if he was still alive. He felt like he was made of Jello. Then he looked at the check and some of his slyness began to return, like a night crawler surfacing in the early hours of the morning. He began wondering if he could take this check to another casino and make it multiply. He rose on shaky legs, but he didn't get far. The entomologist met him at the door and removed the check from his hand. "If you will sign the back, we'll be happy to cash it for you, deduct your losses, pay your bill, and cover the damage you've done to this room," he said.

Steve did as he was told.

Steve's benefactor quietly put the phone down. He had been talking to his friend in Morocco about Steve.

"Steve has become a detriment to our business—in fact, to our very livelihood—and that will be rectified."

"Very well, and do you have an alternate method of transportation?"

"Yes. My son Jonathan will give the particulars to Leila when she gets to New York."

"Very well." Although Leila's father wondered how his friend knew about her.

"Do we need to do anything about this Jared person?"

"If you like to pet cobras, be my guest."

And the conversation ended.

Steve was on his way back to New York, wondering what the hell had happened to him. He wasn't even flying first class. How the hell had he been taken down so badly in only a couple of weeks? He was going to get even. Oh boy, was he ever! He would find Dee, wire her to an anchor, and drop her over the side. Then he remembered he didn't know where his boat was or even where Dee was, for that matter. He was going to get his benefactor's thugs to find Jared and torture him to death while he watched. He smiled at the thought. Then he remembered the briefcase. *Oh shit!* Why hadn't he been contacted? He might have been able to explain why he didn't have it with him. Was that deal gone too?

When he got off the airplane, however, there were two large gentlemen there to meet him. He was escorted to his own penthouse apartment. His benefactor was there with another man Steve recognized as his son, Jonathan. No one was smiling. His benefactor quietly asked Steve for the insurance payment for the month. Steve babbled on that he would have it in a few days when a deal he had in the Mideast went through.

He was told that deal was gone, too. Suddenly he realized there was nowhere to run, nowhere to go. His life had brought him to this. He thought about begging on his knees but knew it wouldn't do any good. His benefactor looked at his son, who nodded his head. The two large gentlemen escorted Steve out of the apartment. The old man explained to his son that when the golden goose starts laying rotten eggs, it's time to find a new goose.

The limo accelerated north on the West Side Highway. Steve knew what was going to happen and he was resigned to it. He knew it was the rule of life and death in his business. A few minutes later the limo turned onto a side road leading down to a lonely spot on the Hudson River. They all got out and Steve's escorts pointed to the end of a sagging pier. Steve walked the length of it with no hope left.

"Don't let me drown," he pleaded.

The two men looked at each other and shrugged. Without a word one held his arms from in front while the other grabbed his shoulders and head from behind and swiftly broke his neck. They wrapped the chains securely around him and dropped him into the water. He never resurfaced. Jonathan walked quickly back to the car without as much as a look back toward the dark water.

Epilogue

I RVING LOOKED UP AT ELLEN as though he had never seen her before. In fact, he never really had seen Ellen like this—ever. The only Ellen he knew was the one who wore boyfriend jeans to work and topped them with baggy tees and sweaters. This Ellen, still wearing her evening gown, was amazingly beautiful and so sexy he was going out of his mind—with worry. In fact, the worry was getting so bad that he was at a loss for words.

"Ellen... look at you! So gorgeous," was all that came out as he stared at her chest, not inches away. And, with that, he tried to reach up to kiss her. Ellen bent down and kissed him with so much enthusiasm he started to fall backwards onto the bed.

"Oh no, this will never do," he muttered. "This will never do."

"Don't you like me, Irving?"

He reclined on the bed in an awkward position. Suddenly he pulled himself up, straightened his clothes, and looked her straight in the eyes.

"Ellen, I like you! I more than like you. I *love* you." Then he stopped and she stared as he started wringing his hands.

"What? Then what's the matter?"

He looked at her with awe and admiration and finally spoke. "You're so beautiful, and I can't ever measure up to your beauty, your experience, how sexy you are... "

"My *experience*? Are you kidding me? Irving! Look at me! Take a good look at me!"

"What?" he wailed. "Look at what, my love?"

"Irving, I don't have any experience. None. I've been a techie geek since junior high. I didn't date. And I intimidated any boy who was interested in me! I'm a VIRGIN! I was counting on you!"

He groaned and buried his head in his hands, and then watched as she let the long white dress slip from her shoulders until she stood in front of him, stark naked. The natural curve of her thigh was right at his eye level.

"We'll figure it out, my darling," she said softly. "I promise we will."

Dee stared at herself in the mirror, unrecognizable in her makeup and dark hair coloring. She began to scrub methodically, hoping the layers of padding and pancake would come off easily. No such luck, she thought. The shower was her only hope, so stripping down, she turned the shower on in the luxurious bathroom and got in. Jared, who had been stretched out on the bed waiting for her, heard the rush of water and went to join her.

"It's no use," she sighed. "There is so much paint on me. It will be in my pores for weeks."

"I know, my darling," Jared said in almost a whisper and pulled her into his arms under the rushing water. "But wasn't it all worth it to actually be there for the big finale?"

"Yes, I guess it was," she mused. "There was so much about Steve I didn't know—didn't even suspect."

"Oh, he was good, Dee. He was very good. No one really knew much about him. He kept to himself. In fact, I'm surprised he ever got married, given how secretive he is. But, enough about Steve. He's part of your past now. And as for your future, here I am!" His grin and the happy look in his eyes told the story.

He turned off the shower jets, stepped out and handed her the largest, softest white towel she could ever imagine. Then, as she wrapped it around herself, he picked her up and carried her to the bed.

He rolled her to him and began to unwrap the towel from her body, toying with her as he went.

"And here's my Christmas present," he said, as her first beautiful breast was revealed, "followed by Valentine's Day, right Dee? I will be allowed a Valentine's Day present, won't I?" This was said as he playfully pulled the rest of the towel from her midsection. He lowered his head and began to kiss and suck, first on one nipple and then the other.

She moaned, her whole body reacting to his ministrations. She reached for his head and brought his mouth down on hers. Now it was Jared's turn to moan as the entire length of her damp and writhing body came in contact with his. She wrapped her legs around him and drew him in, as if she could never get enough of him.

For one second Jared pushed Dee away, just long enough to look at her face. She looked at him with sheer passion. "This is forever, Dee. I love you so much, my darling."

She responded by deepening the kiss and reaching for the wonderful curves of his glorious backside, urging him to enter her.

THE END

We invite you to read a few chapters of **The Penny Scam**, the sequel to **Saving Dee**, which is coming soon.

The Penny Scam

By L. H. Williams

Prologue

THERE WAS A QUIET CHIME, but Ellen and Irving were too busy to hear it. Subconsciously they recorded it, but right now Ellen was astride Irving's recumbent body, gasping for joy. She was riding like an equestrienne at dressage, and when they came to the final gate, they went over it together. And then collapsed in victorious rapture.

When their breathing slowed, and he recovered after a sniff from his inhaler, they looked at each other.

"Was there a… did we have a… " she whispered a little hoarsely.

"I think so," he said, gasping for breath.

Without another word, she unwound her voluptuous form from his gnome-like body and kissed him passionately. Whatever Irving lacked in physical beauty was made up for in the dimension of his "love wand," as Ellen affectionately called it.

They padded naked into their home office and logged onto their computers.

"Oh my, it's XhumeMe," she said. "Remember him?"

"I thought he was still in cyber jail," he answered. "Look at this. He's trying to hack into us."

Ellen's fingers tapped on her keyboard. "He already has. At least he's passed the first level. I've blocked him from going any further."

"I wonder what he wants."

Her fingers flew over her keyboard again.

"He wants us!"

DJ's Confession

DAVID JESSE OWEN, WHO WAS known as DJ, aka "XhumeMe," lit a cigarette from the one he was snuffing out and went back to work on his laptop. He thought the name was clever because it meant "Dig Me Up," as if anyone could find out who he really was. He was wrong. Surrounded by empty takeout containers and dirty ashtrays, he was so far removed from the way he was raised that he was almost unrecognizable. But that didn't bother him—all he cared about was the flickering screen in front of him.

He thought of himself as a modern-day Robin Hood, although he was, by trade, a hacker, and a very successful one at that. But what set him apart from the other hackers was what he called "his gift." He looked around the room at the pictures of his little sister Lisa—lost to him forever when he was ten and she was only six. He remembered how she always sat propped up in her tiny wheelchair and how devastated he was when she died. So, his gift to Lisa came in the form of anonymous donations to any children's charity he could think of. Some of his ideas came from watching television. He'd already adopted numerous orphan girls in Africa and Central America and had sent funds to local children's hospitals; when they asked for a donor's name, if he wrote anything it was always "for my darling Lisa."

It started out small, but as his hacking activities increased, so did his charitable giving. He was making huge amounts of money for his clients, and the "gift skim" was now becoming quite large. It had, in fact, become the latest gossip in charitable circles. He was hacking into the charitable foundations and making large donations. In fact, at one recent luncheon, representatives of five out of six local charities reported discovering anonymous deposits in their bank accounts—one contribution topped fifty thousand dollars.

He stopped working long enough to scan the computers on the tables and desks in his living room, which was his makeshift office. One monitor was running an endless stream of numbers, programmed as it was to find the password he needed to get into one of his clients' accounts.

———————

One of his PCs was generating an inordinate amount of emails, a strange mixture of junk mail and requests from clients for updates to their activities. It sorted it and deleted it at a rate that was unbelievable. This algorithm had taken him almost a month to write and he had thought about selling the rights to Microsoft, but by that time he didn't need the money. Two laptops were devoted to bank accounts, so he could track the progress of both his clients' accounts and his own.

The emails from his key clients generated a special bell, which kept ringing with an insistence he could no longer overlook. It was beginning to annoy him, so he turned his attention in that direction.

The most recent one read: "DJ. Get yr head out of yr ass! We are again short with this operation. Find leak and fix it. If we haf to find it for you, you will be expired."

Oops! DJ decided these messages were getting harder and harder to ignore. Maybe it was time he sought help—before he got "expired."

He thought idly that he was way too young for that.

———————

As Ellen and Irving stood half-naked over the blinking computer screen, another one of their monitors came alive—with a Skype request. Ellen dove for a towel, but it was too late. DJ was already staring at her breasts, and for a second he couldn't seem to speak. But a worried look soon crossed his face and he finally sputtered out what he had to say.

"Where have you two *been*?" he all but howled into his speaker.

Ellen choked back a giggle. "Why you little pipsqueak, DJ. How did you find us? I haven't seen you since I gave that jobs seminar to your high school in Newark. God, that has to be what, six, seven years ago now?"

"Eight," he said, now stony faced.

"Give me a minute, hon, and let me put some clothes on, okay? Keep your pants on, fella."

She could see DJ was rapidly losing his cool, so she tapped Irving on the shoulder and told him to get up off the floor and keep DJ on the phone while she found her wrap.

By the time she wandered back into their computer room, she could see DJ and Irving were deep in conversation, and Irving was all ears. DJ was spilling the beans, and Irving was all but taking notes, he was so interested.

"Okay, kid," said Irving. "Yes, you were right to come to us, and yes, we are the best. But you've got yourself into a bit of a pickle—considering the types you are working with—no, working for. But I think we can help you. Not over the wires, obviously. We'll have to come in person."

Irving motioned for Ellen to take notes. They'd fly in to Newark Airport, then take a taxi to a coffee shop in a tough part of town. "Tomorrow, kid. We'll call your cell phone when we land, okay? And keep your shirt on until then, right?"